HICKEYS AND QUICKIES

by

MaryJanice Davidson

Titles by MaryJanice Davidson

The Undead Series:

Undead and Unwed

Undead and Unemployed

Undead and Unappreciated

Undead and Unreturnable

Undead and Unpopular

Undead and Uneasy

Undead and Unworthy

Undead and Unwelcome

Undead and Unfinished

Undead and Undermined

Undead and Unstable

Undead and Unsure

Undead and Unwary

Undead and Unforgiven

Undead and Done

The Sweetheart Series

Danger, Sweetheart

The BOFFO/FBI Trilogy

Me, Myself and Why

Yours, Mine, and Ours

You and I; Me and You

The Wyndham Werewolves

Love's Prisoner (Secrets, Vol. 6)

Jared's Wolf (Secrets, Vol. 8)

Derik's Bane

Wolf at the Door

The Undersea Folk (mermaids)

Sleeping With the Fishes

Swimming Without a Net

Fish Out of Water

The Déjà *Series (reincarnation)*

Déjà Who

Déjà New

The Alaskan Royals Trilogy

The Royal Treatment

The Royal Pain

The Royal Mess

The Gorgeous Books

Hello, Gorgeous!

Drop Dead, Gorgeous!

The Anthologies

Dying for You

Cravings

(with Laurell K. Hamilton, Rebecca York, Eileen Wilks)

Bite

(with Laurell K. Hamilton, Charlaine Harris, Angela Knight, Vickie Taylor)

Faeries Gone Wild

(with Lois Greiman, Michele Hauf, Leandra Logan

No Rest for the Witches

(with Lori Handeland, Cheyenne McCray, Christine Warren)

Kick Ass

(with Maggie Shayne, Angela Knight, Jacey Ford)

Men at Work

(with Janelle Denison, Nina Bangs)

Dead and Loving It

(with Janelle Denison, Nina Bangs)

Surf's up

(with Janelle Denison, Nina Bangs)

Mysteria

(with P. C. Cast, Gena Showalter, Susan Grant)

Over the Moon

(with Angela Knight, Virginia Kantra, Sunny)

Demon's Delight

(with Emma Holly, Vickie Taylor, Catherine Spangler)

Dead Over Heels

(with P. C. Cast, Gena Showalter, Susan Grant)

Mysteria Lane

(with P. C. Cast, Gena Showalter, Susan Grant)

Perfect for the Beach

(with Lori Foster, Kayla Perrin, Janelle Denison, Erin McCarthy)

The Shorts

Dead But Not Forgotten: Short Stories From
The World of Sookie Stackhouse

My Angel, My Devil

Unwavering

Medical Miracle

Titles by MaryJanice Davidson and
Anthony Alongi

The Jennifer Scales series

Jennifer Scales and the Ancient Furnace

Jennifer Scales and the Messenger of Light

The Silver Moon Elm

Seraph of Sorrow

Rise of the Poison Moon

Evangelina

Welcome to my first ever collection of short stories. And by "collection" I mean three. And by "first" I mean first.

It can be tricky to publish short stories in a conventional paper market, especially little tiny bundles of them. The length is problematic; paper is (comparably speaking) expensive, which is why novellas make more money than shorts. And single titles make more than novellas. But I've always loved the shorter length. Andrew Vachss, one of my favorite authors, explained it perfectly: "Writing short stories is like fighting in a real small ring: whatever your style, you have to get busy quick." (If you've never read him, check out *Flood* or *Strega* or *Blue Belle* to start; they're fine introductions to Burke, Max the Silent, Michelle, the Mole, Mama, and the Prof.)

And that's it right there, what I love best about them. Sometimes you don't want a turkey dinner with mashed potatoes, stuffing, gravy, and cranberry jelly shaped like a can. Sometimes you want one or two pieces of candy. A short story collection is like the truffles in a candy box: trying this flavor won't take long. Or this flavor. Or this one. Except if I carry that metaphor to its logical conclusion, you'll eventually be vomiting truffles because you've gorged yourself on thirty of the rich l'il buggers.

So forget everything you read in this paragraph before you got to this sentence. My metaphor game is way, *way* off today.

Anyhoo, having recently finished my *Undead* series, I was free to try new things (that's probably where I was going with this, right? before I got sidetracked by truffles?), and one of the new things I'm trying is an old thing. All my work, everything I've been able to put on bookshelves or online for readers for the last decade-and-then-some, it all started with writing short stories. It's when I first thought, "If this was my job? I'd be so lucky and so happy." (Spoiler alert: I was right.)

Which brings us to this. The first teeny tiny short story collection. Will there be more? That, dear readers, is entirely on you. And, okay, a tiny bit on me. Like, ten percent on me. Okay, fifteen. Twenty, max. Twenty percent on me, eighty percent on you guys. (My math game is also off.)

Enjoy! Or if you're a new reader who now has an idea of my, um, irreverent writing style and are now experiencing severe buyer's remorse, thanks anyway, and no hard feelings about the return.

MEDICAL MIRACLE

by

MaryJanice Davidson

"Beware; for I am fearless, and therefore powerful." Mary Wollstonecraft Shelley, *Frankenstein*

"There is no such thing as a person that nothing has happened to, and each person's story is as different as his fingertips." Elsa Lanchester

"I'm restless. I can't help it!" Sally, *The Nightmare Before Christmas*

"Start every day off with a smile and get it over with." W.C. Fields

Fun facts:

The Isle Of Man Tourist Trophy is the oldest race in the history of motorcycle racing *and* the most dangerous in the world. In 107 years, over 200 drivers have died. Because we are human, and we like to go fast.

The poster in Vic's office ("Start every day off with a smile and get it over with." W.C. Fields) is a real thing!

You can make a grown-up milkshake with Gerber's baby food, ice cream, and vodka, but I wouldn't recommend it. I honestly think bourbon would be a better choice.

Acrotomophilia, being sexually aroused by people who have had amputations, is also a real thing. No judgement, by the way. Doctors do it for me. And Pop Tarts, for some reason. Chocolate Fudge or Strawberry. If, y'know, you were wondering.

"And the flowers are still standing!" is from the original *Ghostbusters* movie.

Alien Hand Syndrome is another real thing. Let that sink in a minute. *It really happens.* Unfortunately, at this time science knows only enough about the syndrome to scare the crap out of laymen like me, but not enough to fix it. For whatever reason, it most commonly affects the left hand. Also, in case you missed it, *it's real. It is a real thing that happens to actual people in the real world.*

Okay, enough warnings, my work here is done.

Beth Waldman reached with her right hand, the one that had belonged to a driver who died chasing the Isle of Man Tourist Trophy, and shifted to third gear. Most of her had never driven a stick shift before today. But it was proving no trouble. Alarms bypassed: check. Files cracked: check. Anonymous pick-up truck with clean plates: check. (Anonymous trucks, preferably blue, were the John Smith of getaway vehicles: there were so many!)

All this just to return a U-Haul truck a day late; the actual file retrieval hadn't been nearly as complicated. Ridiculous. *Just pay the fine, idiots.*

Flight from MSP to Logan airport: check. Pick up new car from Terminal B garage: check. Check in with lab: ugh.

Still. Had to be done. Standard procedure after every op. Didn't even take that long; D.E.R.P. had it down to a science, pardon the pun. (Wait. *Was* that a pun?)

And so what if she felt like a used car surrounded by indifferent mechanics each time she ran the gamut? Thousands—millions—had it worse. And billions had it much worse; they were in the ground and she should have died in the tunnel. But here she was, alive and well(ish), making good money working a few hours a month. And with free health care, natch. She lived in a beautiful house in Sandwich, she was still walking around on her own two feet.

Well, no. Not really.

The new car had started right up, and as it was 1:00 a.m. on a Wednesday in August, traffic was light. Before long she spotted the Cinnabon shop, pulled off, then pulled in. She parked at the far end behind the lot, grabbed her key card, did a quick mirror-check

(yes, everything's still attached)

and headed for the entrance. It hadn't been a Cinnabon franchise for years, but the place still smelled like the world's most delicious frosting because her life was indefinite and weird (was that redundant?). She could forgive D.E.R.P. a lot, but not ruining Cinnabons for her.

She felt a sudden compulsion to sprint the rest of the way across the lot and hurtle past the checkpoint, and squashed it. She was tired; her day had begun before dawn, she'd chased files all over the city, gotten into two old-fashioned knock-downs (really old-fashioned: the last guy had pulled her hair before he went down—who *does* that outside of elementary school?), and she was tired. So the urge to run and run and run? Wasn't hers.

"Stop it," she muttered at her legs, a strong indicator she was overdue for a psych check. Her left was from a silver medalist— gold? hard to keep track—in the 220 meter hurdles. Her right was from a competitive jogger. Until the last transplant, she hadn't known there was such a thing as competitive jogging. Maybe competitive monkey bars was also a thing. Who knew? *Just once, can I get a transplant from someone who wasn't some kind of pro racer? Or Olympic athlete? Or professional gymnast? Why do people who lived sedentary lives never donate limbs? Why do I never get the hands of a baker or the feet of a shut-in?*

A question for the ages.

She reached the outer door and swiped her card through the magnetic lock. The entrance smelled like pissed-on Cinnabons; now and again they'd "forget" the outer lock and let a random homeless fellow take a leak in there. The smell cut down on traffic and added to the 'yep, totally abandoned space and kinda gross so don't linger!' vibe D.E.R.P. was always going for.

Beth stood still so the *Space For Lease* sign could scan her retina, the least annoying part of the process. She was attached (ha!) to her right eye, the brown one she'd been born with. It didn't do anything special. It wasn't from a fighter pilot with 20/10 vision. She didn't lose it in a poker game. It was just an eye. It was *her* eye.

The first 'a' in *Space For Lease* flashed, and she heard the muted click as the inner door slid aside, revealing an unremarkable elevator. In she went. Nothing fancy, no key card, no armed security guard pointing a Ruger P at her while she recited code words, no trick questions. Just an elevator. Granted, it led to an underground) agency with an eight figure budget and little to no oversight whose outer chamber smelled like pee and frosting, but the elevator itself was nothing special. For some reason, that always disappointed the newbies.

She studied her hands (well...hers temporarily, at least) on the way down. Both donated from small-boned Caucasian women, and the right was a little more weathered than the left. Though she was accustomed to coming at night, it wasn't necessary. The one thing she thought would give her away was the one thing no one seemed to notice. The only one self-conscious about her scars and rotating limbs was her. It sounded asinine, like one of those "these kids today and their <fill in blank>" complaint, but most people were too busy looking down at their phones, or up at whatever screen commanded their attention, to notice her right hand didn't entirely match her left. That her right *anything* didn't always match.

There had been that memorable month when her left leg was from a champion swimmer from Nassau while her right was from a cross-country medalist from Portland. But it had been January in Boston, so no one ever saw her bare legs. It wasn't as if a steady sweetie or a family member would have seen and lost their shit.

No, it wasn't like that was a possibility at all.

The only time her situation had garnered unwanted interest was when a man's left hand was grafted to her wrist for a disastrous ninety-six hours. D.E.R.P. tried to avoid such procedures—the process was tricky enough between non-blood relatives, never mind donors of different sexes. The thing would *not* stop grabbing at her tits all weekend. She put up with a lot, but there were limits. She still remembered calling the lab and politely screaming, "The pervert hand trope? Really? Clear an OR and tell the docs to get scrubbed. I don't care if you have to replace his hand with a garden rake, just get the thing off me!"

Weirdest weekend ever, which was not a phrase she threw around lightly.

The muted 'ding' cut through her thoughts and the doors opened. She stepped out into the sub-sub-sub-basement and managed not to sigh out loud.

"Hey, Beth! Hey, how are ya? Great job, that's what I heard. That thing you did? Which is great. You look great!"

Ben Whitman, who was afraid of her, hid this from himself by overcompensating. Which led to a barrage of over-enthusiastic questions coupled with an inability to make eye contact.

"Hello, Ben." Normally, the Division of Emergency Recovery of Publications' headquarters usually blazed like an operating suite, and was often teeming with suits and lab techs running hither and yon. Sometimes, in addition to hearing the constant, eye-watering hum, you could almost feel the fluorescent lights shining down on you. "Quiet tonight?"

"Sure it is, sure it is." Ben's eyes, pale blue against his near-white blond hair and eyelashes, were showing the whites all around, like a horse who smelled fire. He was tapping the Taser clipped to his belt, probably unconsciously. "Which, y'know, is great. S'far as I know, you were the only agent out and about today, so there's only one tech in the back. Which is great! Who wants a ton of people running around? At night? With most of the lights off? Not us, am I right?"

She decided to mess with him because she was a wretched human being. "Oh, I agree. It's wonderful to have all this space to ourselves. Just you. And me. And one tech who can't even see us."

"Um. Yeah!"

"We could do anything we liked. Raid the fridge. Set files on fire. Go through everybody's in-bins." She had been standing in front of the security bank while she spoke and now leaned forward until she was looming over him. "Nobody would know," she whispered.

Poor Ben made a sound that might have been a laugh. "Right? It's—it's way better that there's only a couple of people here. It's great!" All this as he stared and stared and *stared* at the black band around her neck.

Should have gone with a turtleneck.

She took pity on him and stepped back. "Shall I head back?"

"Sure!" His relief was plain, since she wouldn't see him again until she left. The security staff, to a man/woman, found the labs and operating suites to be unbearably creepy and kept clear. Their job was to keep people from coming back, not actually patrol the back, and they all adhered to the letter of that particular law.

She pushed through the swinging door separating guards from monsters and headed back. The place was decorated in American Office With Cubicles circa 2013: grey cubicles and government-issued beige carpet, white-tiled breakroom with standard fridge, microwave, and drawers full of 300 plastic spoons (but only 7 forks) to the left, restrooms (including the government mandated handicapped stall) to the right. Labs and limb storage

("Aw, c'mon. It's Hypothermic perfusion and—"

"You keep chilly severed limbs in here. Call it what it is, please.")

at the far end. Back here everything looked a lot more expensive (nicer carpet) and high-tech. Actually better than high-tech, because D.E.R.P. defined cutting edge. The cold storage chambers looked like futuristic refrigerators; much of the equipment looked like it was lifted from the set of a *Star Trek* movie. And not a bad one, like *The Final Frontier.* A good one, like *First Contact*.

"Hello?" she tried again.

"Here! I'm here!" Beth heard a distinct thump followed by breaking glass, then hurried footsteps, and then Vic came running. "Sorry! Aw, man, so sorry to keep you waiting." He was shrugging out of his lab coat while he talked, wrestling free of the thing like it had a sentient grip, and while he struggled he tripped and sprawled full-length in front of her.

"Oh, hell," he moaned, face-down on the carpet.

"Are you...all right?" Somehow, she managed to ask this of him with a straight face and without laughing.

"No, I'm mortified."

"I can barely understand you when you mumble into the carpet." *Don't laugh.* "How about turning over?"

"No," he told the carpet. "You'll be annoyed and horrified and you'll leave and I don't want to see any of it." Pause. "This carpet smells really weird."

"I won't be horrified," she promised.

"You might if you smell the carpet." She could hear him actively sniffing. "What *is* that? Did someone dip fried chicken in chocolate, coat it in plastic, and then drop it? Right here?"

"I promise I won't be horrified by anything *you've* done," she amended.

He sighed and flopped over like a salmon dropped on the dock. Victor Clive, lanky cutie and D.E.R.P.'s latest star scientist. She'd only seen him on two other occasions, and then only to nod hello. The second time, she remembered, he took off his lab coat as soon as he saw her. Did he not like lab coats?

He straightened his Clark Kent frames while she reassured him. "See? Still here. Not horrified. Not leaving." She looked around. "They let you fly solo already? I don't think it's ever been so quiet here."

He blinked up at her. "That's not how any of this was supposed to go. Just so you know. I mean, I practiced and everything."

"Pshaw." *I don't think I've said 'pshaw' ever in my life. Why am I busting it out now?* "This sort of thing happens all the time."

"You're lying to set me at ease," he said, still stretched out on the floor. "Which I appreciate, by the way."

She peered down at him, briefly wondered if he was ticklish, squashed the urge to prod a toe into his ribs to find out. "Why did you have to practice?"

His reply, gasped in one sentence, was the last thing she'd expected. "Because I know you hate coming here and hate when everybody stares at you while pretending they aren't so I wanted to make it as comfortable as possible so I fixed it so it's just me this time except for Ben who is scared shitless of you because he's an idiot and won't come back here so you won't have to deal with that, either."

Surprise silenced her. Nothing against the other techs, but she often felt her comfort was secondary to the work. It was a surprise to hear someone flip the priorities.

She looked him up and down again (mostly down), and as on the other two occasions, liked what she saw. He was tall, just over six feet (it was more obvious when he was upright) and slender, but deceptively strong for his body type. The first time she saw him, he had been lugging one of the half-fridges from Point A to Point B without help.

His black hair was short on the sides and long and wavy on top, artfully tousled and thick. His nose was long and sharp, and might have dominated his face if his dark blue eyes hadn't. As with many men, he was blessed with long eyelashes women all over the world tried to duplicate with mascara. Dark stubble bloomed along his jaw and chin and he was blinking at her through black-rimmed glasses. He had dark circles under his eyes—trouble at home? Insomnia? Too much time in the lab? Gambling addiction?

Maybe stop staring and help him up? Right. Good advice; she extended a hand to help him to his feet. When his gaze dropped to the stitches around her wrist, she let go so fast he nearly hit the carpet again.

"Sorry! I am so sorry." She held up her hands in a placating gesture, then remembered the stitches and dropped them again. Fucking Walmart. She'd ordered a half-dozen long-sleeved t-shirt for fall. They sent her three-quarter sleeves because they hated her and wanted her to suffer. And she'd left her jacket in the new car because why wouldn't she? They both knew what she was and why she was here. "Force of habit."

He was already shaking his head. "You've got nothing apologize for. Besides, I'm supposed to see them."

Right. Because this wasn't a date. It wasn't even a meet cute. He was a mechanic, and she was the car that needed new tires. Or windshield wipers. Or whatever the hell. Metaphors weren't her strong suit.

"Okay then!" He'd bounded back to his feet and actually bounced up and down a little. "Let's get started so you can get the hell out of here."

She snorted and followed him toward the exam rooms. "You enjoy my company that much?"

"No!" He stopped, horrified, and actually slapped his forehead. "Stupid, *stupid.* That's not what I meant. I love your company. I mean—I don't mind it. You. I don't mind your—I *love* your—uh—"

She'd thought he was about her age at first—late twenties?—but his energy made him seem younger. "Maybe we should just begin."

"Right! Beginning is good. It's just this way." And he darted off like a setter intent on flushing pheasant.

"Yes, I remember." *Argh, quit it. He's adorable, quit poking at him.*

I will if he will, she snapped back at herself. *But he won't. There's going to be plenty of poking, and none of it the fun kind.*

Because here was Vic Clive, a thoughtful, enthusiastic, handsome genius, and all she could think about was: he was going to see her scars and pretend she wasn't a freak stitched together from dead people. At best, he'd see her as an interesting lab rat. At worst, a living ghoul.

Either way: not sexy, or even lovable. And that was fine. She knew what she'd signed up for. She could have succumbed to her wounds and died, like a sensible person.

She paused when he went left instead of right, and followed him to the end of another hallway and into a cold sterile exam room that looked like...

"Eh?"

...a comfortable office decorated in Lair Of The Geek?

He turned and saw her surprise. "Is this okay? You're not here for the full check-in."

She had hoped, but wasn't sure until he said it. "Really?"

"You just had one ten days ago. And going by the reports, you didn't suffer significant trauma this time."

Okay, not that she was arguing, but... "One of them pulled my hair. I don't like people touching my hair." She folded her arms across her chest and knew it was childish, but couldn't stop herself. "It's *mine*."

He held up his hands in a 'please don't hit me' pose. "I don't blame you. I wouldn't like some corporate spy yanking my hair, either."

"Nonsense." She smirked. "They could never get a grip, not with all the hair product you favor."

"I'll thank you," he said with exaggerated dignity, "to keep your snide commentary of my personal hygiene to yourself." He reached up and felt the crown of his head. "Which reminds me, I'm almost out...never mind. All joking aside, it's still just a standard check, just vitals and such. So I figured here'd be okay. Unless you'd rather—?""

"This is fine." 'This' was a room with lots of low, warm light but not a fluorescent to be seen, overstuffed chairs in front of the desk which wasn't a desk, but a long table piled with files, empty Subway wrappers, books. Bookshelves lined the far wall, everything from *Operative Techniques in Transplantation Surgery* to *The Sandman* graphic novels. There was a small brown fridge in the corner just below the "Start every day off with a smile and get it over with" poster, which he went to at once, opened, grabbed something, turned. She had to smile: he was holding out a bottle of sweet tea, her non-alcoholic tipple of choice.

"Thank you," she said, then guzzled with the finesse of a cow at the water trough. She only then realized how thirsty she was. Her body couldn't process heavy food—steak dinners and the like were permanently off the menu—which meant a liquid diet supplemented with broth and baby food. The most annoying part was how much she liked some of the baby food. Gerber's pureed peaches? Divine.

Especially when you threw a couple of jars of it in a blender with ice cream and vodka.

He'd grabbed a bottle for himself and they clinked them together. She had to laugh. "This is the closest thing I've had to a date in years."

Vic nearly choked on his tea and for a moment she wondered if she'd have to pound him on the back. "Oh, sure," he managed, eyes watering. "Like that's at all believable."

"It's true," she protested. "I haven't been on a date in years." Four, in fact. She'd waited until two years after the accident and the subsequent surgical procedures. Dinner and a movie had been almost as big a disaster as the accident that should have killed her.

"Really?" Vic was still shaking his head. "Well, I guess if you're so busy saving the world—"

"I have never once saved the world," she pointed out. "I've never even saved a city block."

Still with the head-shaking. "Some of those files, if they'd fallen in the wrong hands—"

She waved that away. "I sometimes turn the tables on companies that indulge in corporate espionage. That's it. That's all it is."

"You're not giving yourself enough credit. What you do—it's important. If for no other reason than we can use the profits to—to—" He gestured at her. "To do all these wonderful things. We've advanced amputee rehabilitation and organ transplants by *decades*."

"But only for a select few," she pointed out. She wasn't D.E.R.P.'s only monster, just their first. If J.A.M.A. or the New England Journal of Medicine caught on to what they were up to, they would, as the saying went, collectively flip their shit.

"For now, yes." He set his drink on the table behind him—one of those people who liked to talk with their hands. "But clinical trials will start soon. Now that we've broken the 72-hour time threshold and figured out a way around the inevitable anoxia and toxin accumulations, the— okay, I know it's a cliché, but the sky really is the limit. Because of you."

Ah, no. He was giving credit to the limbs, not the people who sewed them on. But if he wanted to see her that way, she wasn't going to argue. This had already been one of the nicest experiences she'd ever had at Not-Cinnabon.

With his hands free, she was amused to note, he talked even faster. "...and, of course, cold storage—"

"The old," she observed.

"—paired with artificial perfusion—"

"The new."

"—has revolutionized the industry. Shit, there goes another cliché."

"I don't mind. Essentially, what you're saying is, 'Eureka!'" (Because "It's alive! It's aliiiiive!" was already taken.)

Still, clinical trials were an important third step, if lengthy. Inevitably, they'd be able to get around The National Organ Transplant Act of 1984. Everything would change. To what extent, she could not be sure, but that was because in her former life, she'd been an accountant. Even now, after several procedures, she wasn't entirely sure how the process worked. Unprecedented medical breakthroughs coupled with a fundamental understanding of blah-blah-blah, nanotech and molecular-scale electronics something-something, and that's where they lost her, every time. And her confusion was no fault of D.E.R.P.'s. They had tried, many times, to explain exactly what they did and are doing and how it worked and what would happen next. For her part, she decided it was medical sorcery and hadn't entirely discounted the dark arts, either.

"Thank you," she said. "It's good to be reminded that there's value to this, that people's lives will change for the better."

He nodded so hard he had to push his glasses back up. "It's why I wanted to work here," he said simply. "It's all I ever wanted. Um. This is gonna seem hokey, but..." He'd reached back, found his phone, made a few swipes, and showed her a picture of a smiling woman in a wheelchair, with coal black skin, large and lovely eyes, and a smile that could only be described as dazzling. She had one arm hooked around Vic's neck. The other arm had been taken at the elbow, and both legs were missing at the knee.

"She's gorgeous."

"Yeah. We were in the same accident when we were kids, only she wasn't wearing her seat belt." When she looked up, he added, "My big sister."

"Your—oh?"

"What?" he teased, taking back his phone. "You don't see the family resemblance?"

"Well, no, since you're about as dark as a grub." His eyebrows arched and he laughed, *thank God*, because she couldn't believe she'd just compared him to beetle larva. Anxious to move the topic from grubs, she added, "I won't deny being envious. I was a ward of the state, so. No family."

Vic nodded. Few ties (preferably zero ties) to family and friends was a program requirement. A short silence fell, broken by his polite, "Would you like more tea?"

"No, thank you."

"All right." He reached past her and snagged something off one of the piles of paper on his desk/table. "Let's get started. You want to get home, I know."

She eyed the clipboard. "How quaint."

"Right? It's a classic."

"Like a Ford Capri."

"Exactly like that," he deadpanned. "I was just telling myself that this clipboard was a lot like an old car." He was taking her pulse, then carefully feeling her wrist, her elbow, her shoulder. Then he switched to the other hand, wrist elbow, shoulder. "Any circ problems?"

"My circulation is fine, thank you." She knew he'd ask that straight off; it was always their biggest concern. She'd pulled her stupid three-quarter sleeve t-shirt over her head so he could auscultate, and stood before him patiently while he did. Her fingers went to the snap on her jeans and he stopped her. "That's not necessary this time. No needed to poke, prod, bore, *and* make you cold."

"You're not boring me."

"Well, thank God for that." His hands were on her face now as he checked her sclera for discoloration (white = good, yellow or black = bad), then grabbed his retinoscope for a closer peek. He took her blood pressure, which was ridiculously low and always had been—as a child, she used to sneak into the kitchen to devour salt right out of the shaker. Low BP was another D.E.R.P. requirement. He checked her ears, then set the instrument aside and inspected the stitch marks at her wrists and elbows, then palpated her temporomandibular joint and lymph nodes. He rested his fingers on her collarbones for a second, then asked, "May I?" and gestured to her throat.

Oh.

That.

Her fingers flew to the dark band around her neck. It was a black strip just under an inch wide, deceptively strong, and attached at the nape with tiny snaps that were difficult to open without practice. It would never accidentally unsnap. No one could get it off in less than thirty seconds without her help.

She never took it off unless she was alone. Or here, in this place.

"I have to look," he said gently. "I won't hurt you."

She snorted. "I'm not remotely worried about you hurting me." Then she reached behind her head and unsnapped the band. He paused, giving her a couple of seconds, and then his warm fingers carefully felt the scar.

"Looks good," he commented. "It's healed up nicely. No keloids. If people didn't...you know, if they didn't know, they wouldn't know, you know?"

"I don't know what's worse, that you said that or that I understood it." But she smiled. He reached up, felt behind her ears where there'd be a scar if she'd had a face-lift (which, in a way, she supposed she had, a very fucking severe face-lift), felt the scar at the base of her neck, and she shivered.

His fingers stilled. "Sorry."

"Tickles," she managed, and for some reason that got them both giggling. His eyes, she decided, really were the most perfect shade of dark blue, like wet denim. She liked them, especially when they were...were...

Oh, now that's interesting...

It wasn't just their color catching her attention, but the size of his pupils. They were enormous, she realized, with a dark blue sliver around the edge. And it wasn't the lighting. It wasn't operating room bright in his office, but it wasn't a murky cave, either. And she could tell he wasn't afraid of her, like Ben and some of the others were.

To be fair, she didn't do much to alleviate their fears. She probably shouldn't have teased them when she saw them smoking in the back lot. ("Arrgh! The villagers have come with fire! Rrrraaaawwwrr!") One of those things that had been funnier in her head than in execution. But what idiot under the age of 30 smoked in this day and age?

Never mind them. Concentrate on him. On his eyes. It's not too dark in here. He's not scared of me. He's not drunk. Or stoned—not with all the random piss tests around here. So that leaves...

She reached out and took his hands in hers. "You made sure you were on duty when I came in."

He broke eye contact and stared at the floor. "Luck of the draw. Whim of the scheduling gods."

"You tossed your lab coat the second you realized I was here."

"It gets hot in here. All the, uh, fridges. The equipment. It gets warm."

"Nice try, but we both know the temp here is permanently set to 'you need a parka'. You also," she continued, "made a point of bringing me back to your comfortable and decidedly unthreatening office."

"All my stuff's in here. And my Skittles."

"You have treated me with respect bordering on—" Reverence. At least, that's how it felt. Like she was precious to him, and not necessarily because of anything she had done, or could do. Which couldn't be right, but still: it *seemed* like it could be. For lack of a better word, or more data, she'd stick with reverence.

She took a breath and plunged. "Would you like to have dinner?"

He looked up, eyes widening. "Yes please."

"With me?"

He gave her a look. "Of course with you."

"Don't get pissy because I'm a stickler for detail," she said, which set them both off.

"I like your white streaks," he said out of nowhere, gesturing toward her short (mostly) dark hair.

"It's my homage to Elsa."

"What, like in *Frozen*?"

"Um. No."

He grinned. "Sorry. Messing with you a little."

"Just for that, you can pay for dinner."

"I'll pay for anything you want. Can we go right now?" he joked, then sobered when she didn't say anything. "It's okay. I know you're tired. Anytime you want to go, I'm up for it. Anywhere. That's all I'm saying. Just give me a date and a place and a time. I'll be there. Have I emphasized that I'll be there? I feel like I'm not emphasizing that enough. I want you to know that I'll be there."

"I *was* tired," she said slowly. "Not now, though." In fact, she felt more "it's aliiiiiive!" then she had for years. "I'm not hungry, either. Well, I am, but not for food." *Argh. So hokey. Never mind. Keep going*. "So perhaps we should dodge the preliminaries and get to it."

And she leaned in and kissed him on his sweet, surprised mouth. For a terrifying second he didn't move, didn't return the kiss, didn't react at all. Just as she started to pull back and offer an embarrassed apology (then run away and find a cave to live in for the rest of her life, periodically emerging to terrorize villagers and hiss at the sunshine), his hand came up, cupped the back of her neck, and he kissed her back.

This is insane.

Yes. But dammit, the brain was hers, and the skull, and the hair, even if nothing else was. And her brain was telling her—yelling at her—to take him*, for God's sake, it's been so long, what do you need, a Friend request? Take him!*

"Oh my God," he managed against her lips, and then both hands were on her and he was stepping close, walking her backward until her back hit the wall. "Oh my God, you have no idea. How much. How long I've. Thought. About doing this." Each pause was punctuated with another kiss.

"Really?" She was hearing his words, she was sensing his intent, his desire was beyond obvious, but it was still amazing to hear. "Why didn't you say anything?"

"How could I? It's way past inappropriate. Not to mention creepy. 'Hey, I saw your horrific accident on TV and followed your case and came to work here hoping to meet you and kind of have a crush now and I've read all your files and am a tiny bit obsessed, wanna go out sometime?'"

She pulled back. "That would have worked."

He chuckled. "I didn't know." He kissed her clavicle, the base of her throat, her scar. Nuzzled the side of her neck as she reached up and ran her fingers through his hair. *Hmm. Good hair product. No sticking!* "How could I know? You're a walking talking medical miracle, you endured crushing injuries, made hard choices, and then had an unprecedented recovery which took strength of will I can barely imagine, then obligingly put yourself in danger to help companies fend off corporate espionage."

She was already shaking her head. "That's not...how it was." He was making getting caught on the wrong end of the Big Dig tunnel collapse and buried for five hours sound almost noble, instead of a result of piss-poor planning. *I didn't even have to drive to Logan that day! I had a T-pass, for God's sake.*

"I saw the pictures. That's exactly how it was. Beth, you're smart and strong and lovely and—no, don't, I said lovely," as she'd opened her mouth to ruin a good thing by protesting again. "I don't give a shit whose limbs you're wearing on any given day, or who this—" Tapping her stomach. "—used to belong to. Well, I do give a shit, but only in terms of being grateful to all your donors."

"Muh," was all she could come up with. *Do better.* "Wha?" *Argh.*

"It's you. You're who I want. It's your mind and your heart I lo—admire." He cleared his throat. "The latter is obviously figurative and not literal."

"Damn," she marveled. "How did you manage to make 'figurative' sound erotic?"

He smiled. "My point, which stands, is that you could be with anybody. So it never occurred to me that you'd be interested, never mind that you'd return an inappropriate and unprofessional and ethically questionable advance."

"Shows what you know. Inappropriate and unprofessional is my kink. Well, that and ice cream floats, but that's a whole other conversation. Besides, all those things apply to you." She tipped her head back to allow better access, because one of three things was happening. He either didn't notice her scars (impossible), didn't care (perhaps), or they turned him on because he had a touch of acrotomophilia. *None of those are a deal-breaker, so proceed.* "Except for the part where you're a medical miracle, but you could swap that out for 'genius', and *you* could be with anybody."

"Yeah, but..." He gestured to her. "It's like I said. You're who I want. Who I've wanted. For years."

"Fuck dinner." She was working open his shirt buttons and reminding himself not to yank, not to send buttons flying everywhere. Someone could lose an eye, and then *urgh*, more surgery. "Fuck me instead."

"Yes please," he groaned as he cupped her ass through her jeans. She'd gotten the shirt unbuttoned and yanked it off him like a magician doing the tablecloth trick.

("And the flowers are still standing!")

Then she attacked the button on his pants while Vic tried to remove her sports bra, kiss her, kick off his shoes, and run his hands all over her at the same time.

"Your multitasking sucks," she informed him.

"Sorry," he gasped, finally reliving her of her bra. She brushed his hands aside, toed off her flats, shucked off her jeans, and muttered an inaudible prayer of thanks that she'd had time to shower and change clothes before her flight.

"I like these," she said of the gray boxer briefs. "But let's lose 'em anyway."

"Whatever you want," he promised as she pushed them down to his ankles, helped him step out of them, decided his socks could stay (for now). "I'll lose anything you say. *Do* anything you say. Just tell me because oh my God, your hands. Keep doing that, please, and don't worry if I dissolve."

She'd run the tips of her fingers through his neatly trimmed pubic hair, then reached for his cock, long and slender, flushed deep red at the tip, already beading pre-come. She ran her thumb over the slick head, felt the weight of it, stroked the underside, then tightened her grip for a couple of firm strokes. "Like that?"

"Hhhnnngg."

"Or that?"

"This might kill me. You might actually murder me and I am *fine* with that."

"So accommodating," she teased.

"Yes. My middle name is accommodating. Whatever you need. Anything to, uh, lighten the load."

She groaned. "Terrible." He reached for her panties, started inching them down her hips. "But I'll forgive you this once and what do you think of the couch?"

"You like it? Ikea. Easy to assemble."

"I wasn't looking for a ConsumerAffairs review."

"Right. Of course. The couch. Definitely." They were sort of sidling/shuffling over to the thing, more intent on kissing and stroking than actual momentum. As far as Beth was concerned, they could do it on a cot. A pool float. On top of the table. Under the table. Who cared? She just wanted to get prone. She felt the backs of her legs hit the vinyl—leather?— couch and went down

"Aaggh! Cold!"

tugging Vic on top of her. His heavy warmth was as reassuring as it was sexy. "*God, you feel good*," he gulped, hands roaming while he nuzzled the slopes of her breasts. "But we can't."

"What?" She had both hands on his ass, which was delightfully springy beneath her fingers. She wanted to dig in, wanted to mark him, wanted to scratch *Beth Waldman was here* on his cheeks with her fingernails. And maybe underline it. "Why?"

He groaned and dropped his forehead to her shoulder. "We can't. We shouldn't do this because something-something unethical something else." When she blinked up at him, he managed, "I know there are actual and relevant real-world reasons why we shouldn't do this, I just can't remember any of them."

"That is, honest to God, one of the nicest things anyone has said to me in four years. Fuck ethics and fuck appropriate. I'll sign a waiver if that'll relieve your ethical dilemma, just let me suck your cock and then ride it for a while, okay? Frankly, Vic, I don't think that's too much to ask."

"It's pretty reasonable."

"Good. Get up here." He got to his knees, then slowly shuffled up the length of the couch until his cock was hanging just a couple of inches from her mouth. She smiled. "Even better. Oh, and grab onto something. It'll be a few minutes."

"I love you. Sorry, I meant to say you don't have to hhhhhaaaannnnnggggg..."

It wasn't about 'have to'. It was about 'get to'. She'd always loved this part of sex, for reasons that were only partly altruistic. She didn't just enjoy having a man put something precious within her reach (literally), or hearing the groans and moans and wonderful sexy sounds she could coax out of someone with her lips and tongue and fingers. The act itself got her wet, made her hungry, made her want and *want*. The only thing she could think of when she had a cock down her throat was how much better it would be to have that same cock somewhere else, somewhere tighter and warmer.

"Beth—you—you're—ah—ah—"

It was also necessary for a more practical reason. She hadn't brought lube to her check-in (why *would* she?), so she was going to need something to pave his way, so to speak. She could get wet, just like she could bleed or cry or sweat. But it took longer, so she hoped he'd made himself comfortable.

So she licked and sucked and played with his balls, grinned at the glorious sounds she was wringing out of him, encouraged him to thrust, writhed beneath him as his need kindled her own, and after a lovely long time she pulled off and said, "Now. I want you in me right *now*."

She could have laughed at his dazed expression, the flush that started at his forehead and went down his chest, his panting. She wouldn't, though it wouldn't have been to mock him. She wanted to laugh for the sheer joy of making him look like that, feel like that, sound like that. But laughing and explaining why she was laughing would rob them of valuable fucking time.

He moved back, settled between her thighs, kissed her long and hard, began to ease into her. She propped her left leg up on the back of the couch, spread herself further for him, and a sigh escaped him as he bottomed out.

"Okay? Is this okay?"

She could barely understand him, his voice was so thick, and wasn't *that* exciting? "Exceptionally okay—*ohhhhh*, that's nice." He was moving carefully, watching her face, brushing her hair out of her eyes with trembling fingers. "It doesn't hurt at all. Don't stop."

"Thank God," he muttered into her neck, and she laughed. He was moving easily now, and she was raising her hips and meeting every thrust. It occurred to her that not only was his office door unlocked, it was open. That should have mortified her, or at least worried her, but she couldn't muster the energy for it. Ben wouldn't come near them, that was one thing. She didn't care if someone caught them, that was another. They'd earned this, that was a third.

She felt the tell-tale tightening in her mid-section, her body's precursor to orgasm, and was amazed. Even with five minutes of head, she never came this quickly. Even in her own body, she'd never come so fast. "I'm close. I can't believe it, but—yes. Can you...? Harder? I'm almost—yes! Just like that, please don't s-stop."

"I won't," he panted, "but could you try to look a little less delicious? And sound a little less hot? Because I'm. Almost there. Too."

"No promises," she warned, then cried out at the ceiling. She'd gone from 'I'm going to come' to 'wow, I'm coming' in next to no time. "God, that's good, that's so good, now you, oh please please..."

"I can feel it," he groaned, smearing kisses all over her mouth as he bucked into her. "God, I can—all your muscles just contracted around me, it's—*fuck*."

His eyes rolled back and she realized he still had his glasses on, which struck her as hilarious and cute. Then he was shaking through the after-effects of what looked like a spectacular orgasm, so she reached up and carefully pulled the frames off his face.

"Huh," he managed between gasps as she set them aside. "Right. I wear glasses. To correct my vision. Which I should have taken off. Or something."

She grinned. "Don't worry. I'm taking it as a compliment. Or that you're just really forgetful."

"Thanks for that. Also, that was fucking phenomenal and I want to take you out to dinner for real and then if I am, in fact, the most fortunate man on the planet right now, which I'm pretty sure I am, I'm hoping you'll consent to bouncing on my cock for a while. Ever since you said that, I haven't been able to—I mean, I *just* came, but all I can think about is coming again. With you. After dinner."

She pretended to think it over and realized he was literally holding his breath as he waited for an answer. "I think that sounds great. I think that sounds like dessert. I think I could eat a dozen jars of pureed peaches right now, after which I'd be delighted to sit on your cock." She was already thinking about smearing puree all over him and licking it off. And not just peaches. Pears. Apples. Bananas. Whatever. Gerber alone offered 40+ kinds of fruit.

"Really?" He propped himself up on an elbow and smoothed her hair out of her eyes. "So this isn't just a one-nighter? Not that I'd complain," he hastened to add. "But I'd be lying if I said I wasn't hoping for more."

"Me, too. 'Hoping for more' is how I got into this mess to begin with. I wasn't ready to die. Not over a tunnel collapse I had no business being near. 'Hoping for more' worked for me then. And now." She reached up, brushed her thumb over his cheekbone. "Right now."

He caught her fingers, kissed the tips, cleared his throat. "By the way, your check-in went fine. Flying colors and all that. I'll cc you on the chart paperwork."

She blinked at the ceiling. "That's a load off my mind."

"Isn't it, though?"

They giggled—she'd laughed more in the last twenty minutes than in the last month—then unpeeled themselves from each other and the couch (a disadvantage of couch sex), found their clothes, cleaned up a little, got dressed, shut down the light banks.

In next to no time, they were waving good-bye to Ben

("Oh, you're going? Both of you? Now? And won't be back? At least for tonight? Okay, great! Bye!")

and stepped into the elevator. "Come to my place," he coaxed. "Will you? Tonight? After we have dinner?"

"Of course. But you must be starving. And—forgive me, but you look tired." She leaned up, moved his glasses, kissed the dark shadows under each eye, settled his frames back in place. "How long since you slept?

"I always stay here when you're in the field, until I know you're—" He trailed off and treated her to a bashful shrug. "Well. You know."

You just earned yourself another five minute blowjob, you clever, clever man.

"So let's just get take-out or something," she urged, "and go to your place, and eat, and sleep, and the afore-mentioned cock bouncing can also happen, and then perhaps a nap followed by breakfast."

"I...might be in love with you."

"That's fine."

"Also, I really want a Cinnabon." He yawned. "I know. Stupid. But I've had the worst craving for the last two days."

"That's all right. You can have the bread, and I'll have the frosting."

"Perfect," he declared as he followed her out of the elevator.

"No. Weird as fuck. But it seems that might work for us."

"It does seem like that," he agreed, and kissed her as the doors slid shut.

THE END

UNWAVERING

by

MaryJanice Davidson

"Uneasy lies the head that wears a crown." William Shakespeare, *Henry IV, Part 2*

"Hell is empty. All the devils are here." William Shakespeare, *The Tempest*

"I hate Shakespeare. I think Shakespeare is rubbish." Allan Carr

"What's the point of these quotes at the beginning of a story, anyway?" Random reader

This story takes place a few months after the events of *Undead and Done.*

New to the Undead series? No problem. (Don't worry, there won't be a quiz.)

Long story short (unlike every other time someone says 'long story short', this long story will actually be short), Betsy Taylor, whose love for designer shoes is an all-encompassing hunger, gets fatally smashed by a Pontiac Aztec while looking for her cat.

She wakes up dead, escapes the morgue, keeps all her old friends, makes new friends, repeatedly cheats death, and comes to realize she's the long-foretold vampire queen. Violence happens. Also sex. Then more violence. And even more sex. Along the way, Betsy gets into a prolonged catfight with Satan (who looks like Lena Olin in a gray designer suit). The end result? Betsy takes over the care and feeding of Hell and its billions of denizens. (Nametag: "Hello, My Name Is Satan 2.0") Then more sex.

See? Easy. But you'll be okay either way, you can read this story without having so much as peeked at an Undead book. Though you really should. It's a pretty fun series, if I do say so myself.

Sex?

Or shoes?

In what twisted world would I have to choose?

Ha! I was a poet and I didn't know it. I have layers, y'know. There's more to me than a pretty face and an eternally 30 year-old body and a magnificent closet and the whole queen thing and the ruling Hell gig.

(What? There is!)

"Oh my God, *Elizabeth Frankenstein Taylor*!"

"What? What?" I straightened up in such a hurry, I almost fell off the kitchen stool. "Are you okay? Are we under attack?" I looked wildly around the kitchen. "Did you lose your phone again?"

"I have been talking to you for five minutes about tonight and you've been gaping at me with your mouth open muttering 'sex' and 'shoes' for almost that long."

"Okay, Marc, but...don't call me Elizabeth." What had my mother been thinking? Who stares down at a newborn and says, 'welp, no need to think about this one second longer, let's go with Elizabeth Taylor because no one will ever tease her'? "And we've been over this—my middle name isn't Frankenstein."

The zombie's (chilly) hands settled on my shoulders and yeah. It was a little alarming. He bent in close. Dentist close. Or doctor close, which made sense—Marc was an M.D. "When my face is pointed at you and sounds are coming out of my mouth hole, that's usually an indication that I'm talking to you and would like your attention."

I wriggled free from his clammy grip. "Usually?"

"Sometimes I'm just bitching," he allowed. "Under the right circumstances, it's better than Valium."

"Right. Look, I'd love to hang and chat about whatever it is—"

"Lying!" he declared. "You are looking me in the face and telling bald-faced falsehoods and would be dead to me if you weren't already."

"—but today is a special day. It's—" I broke off and listened. "Ooh!"

"You look like Petey the dog when you cock your head like that."

The kitchen door swung open, revealing my tall, dark, handsome husband. Eric Sinclair, king of the vampires and ruler of my cold, sporadically beating, undead heart.

"Oooh, ooh!" It was downright embarrassing how just the sight of my husband reduced me to things like "oooh!" It's also possible I might have jumped up and down a little.

Sinclair beamed. "My own."

Marc let out an inelegant snort. Which is probably redundant. (I don't think it's possible to elegantly snort.) "I think you should've waited until the sun was at your back, Eric, it would have been way more dramatic. Go out and try again."

"Don't listen to Marc," I said. "He's grumpy about...uh..." What had it been? Something about pads. Or heat? Did he want potholders? Or some of those big puffy oven-

safe mittens? I'd buy him a thousand.
Just...later.

"I'm sorry to hear that, Marc," Sinclair
murmured. The kitchen door was swinging shut
behind him as he advanced on me like a big cat.
A lion, maybe. Or a sexy ocelot.

"I haven't actually told you my problem,"
was the aggrieved reply. "And Betsy didn't,
either. Which, in itself, is kind of the problem."

"I have every confidence the situation will
be resolved to your satisfaction," Sinclair
continued, and it wasn't fair. It just wasn't. Tall
and gorgeous *and* brilliant *and* sexy *and*
dynamite in bed (literally! we did it next to a pile
of sparklers last 4th of July). He was an
embarrassment of riches.

But the strangest thing about my
husband? Besides his predilection for baking
homemade dog treats for our puppies, Fur and
Burr? He thought I was irresistible, too. Which
made *no* sense, but I sure wasn't going to argue.

"I hate you," someone—Marc, I wanted to
say?—was whining, "almost as much as I hate
your wife."

Then Sinclair was right in front of me,
sliding his big hands past my waist, down the
backs of my thighs, and then he lifted me to him
like I weighed as much as a damp handkerchief.

Take it from a gal who has been six feet tall since the eighth grade: when a guy effortlessly picks you up, it's so. Fucking. Hot.

Then—whoosh! The kitchen door was swinging again. And we were on the right side this time.

"Wait! You never told me where annnnnnd they're gone."

"Marc required your assistance?"

By now I was resting my head on Sinclair's chest so I could feel his deep voice rumble out. "I don't know, how should I know? Faster, please. We have to go faster because our stupid bedroom is two floors and at least a thousand feet away so faster, right now—faster!"

"That's not what you urged last night," he teased.

"Really? You're trying a 'that's what she said' thing? Stick to 20th century humor, pal."

"I suppose such things are...ah...better left to experts." The 'ah' because I'd worked open some of the buttons on his deep blue Royal Oxford shirt and was licking the exposed skin. (This was Sinclair at his most casual: dress shirt, slacks, belt, socks—but no jacket or tie, the hedonist.) He set me carefully on my feet and leaned against the bannister to give me some wiggle room. So I did what any right-thinking horny vampire would do: pounced on him. If he was a sexy ocelot, I was a sensual bobcat!

"Too many buttons," I whined.

"The three words I treasure most from your lips, darling."

"I'll give you three words," I muttered, losing patience and jerking his shirt free of his pants.

"*There* you are!"

I spun and beheld my friend Jessica holding the Ultimate Mood Breakers™: her cute weird babies.

"What now?" I snapped.

"Ex*cuse* me?"

"Sorry. I meant 'oh look who stopped by and brought us her weird cute babies without calling first'."

"I haven't called before coming over for fifteen years! On *your* instructions, after the Miss Congeniality debacle."

Ugh. Don't remind me. Sullying that pageant was my worst act before I died. Or my finest, depending on where you land on the "are pageants great or terrible" spectrum.

"And they have names, y'know." Jessica sounded the way she usually did when we got into it: exasperated-yet-fond. Or maybe it was the other way around. We'd been friends since junior high and she was one of those terrible women who didn't age. She still had the same dark, perfect complexion, the same big beautiful eyes, the same perpetually surprised expression (she liked pulling her hair back—*way* back— which made her eyebrows arch). And mere months after popping out the twins, she was back to her scrawny-skinny frame. So aggravating. "And you'd better not be calling them weird babies when they're in high school, Betsy."

She was in full Aggravated Mom mode (far more terrifying than Irritated Roommate mode), pacing back and forth (she only ever paced three feet forward and three feet back, so it was like watching a wind-up toy with a great manicure) with a beautiful bright-eyed baby on each hip watching us with interest. "Your mom asked me to swing by and grab some of BabyJon's toys so he could play with the twins. And what thanks do I get, coming here out of my way?"

"No thanks?" I guessed (seemed safest).

"*No* thanks!" Jessica was wearing her usual collection of comfortable faded clothing (long-sleeved red t-shirt, black jeans, sandals and *argh*, the state of her toenails!), all liberally decorated with baby formula. (How do you even get baby formula on your feet?) The good news was, the formula set off her dark skin in a really superb way. Except for the only four hours of sleep a night thing, motherhood had been great for my oldest and best friend.

"But don't worry," she was continuing, because even if she suspected I'd tuned her out, she figured Sinclair, at least, would be paying attention. Foolish woman! Sinclair was only thinking about my pants, specifically: how to divest me of them. "We won't be here long, so you two horny toads can get back to humping on the stairs and good God, man!" Jessica had stopped in mid-pace. The babies were also goggling at Sinclair. "What happened to your shirt?"

Sinclair looked down and seemed surprised to behold that his shirt below the second button was shredded. He looked part man, part carwash mop. "To begin," he said with convincing dignity, "the queen and I never 'hump'. We—"

"Spare me the perv details."

"It is," he continued, a neat trick with the shreds of his shirt fluttering around his knees, "a special day for us."

"Oh, because you're about to do a hallway bang?" She giggled and one of the babies did, too. The other was focused on devouring its hand. Not part of the hand. *The whole hand.* I didn't know if I should discourage or cheer. I also didn't know which one was the boy or the girl since Jessica refused to slap a Hello My Name Is sticker on their tiny shirts. (Because she was an unreasonable harridan.) "You guys have a lot of special days."

"Yep, it's all special all the time around here so we'd better get back to it."

"Nice to see you, Jessica!" Jessica yelled, because that was her idea of subtle.

"Well, it was."

"We miss you around here, Jessica!"

"Well, we do."

"Jerks." This in a tone of restrained affection, and, formalities finished, she was bustling past us and up the stairs toward my brother/son's room. (Long story short, my father and stepmother had a baby together. They're gone now. The baby remains. We're the *real* modern family, what with brother/sons and zombies and vampires and puppies and the occasional ghost all under one roof.) Sinclair turned to follow (we had to; our room was up those same stairs) and I hopped on his back, because he's super strong and I'm nimble like that.

But I forgot about physics. Sinclair clutched for the banister, missed, and we both tumbled backward and fell.

(Fuck you, physics.)

"Elizabeth!"

"Argh, I'm squashed like a bug." I groaned and elbowed him off me. He obliged and I heard him swallow a snort of laughter as he rolled to his feet and beheld my flattened form. "Not funny."

"No, of course not." He bent, took my hand, helped me to my feet. "It was churlish to laugh."

"The churlishest," I agreed. "Let's totter up the stairs like the geezers we'll eventually be, then bang like bunnies once we're on the right side of a closed bedroom door."

Ah, my own, you read my mind.

That's literal, by the way. It wasn't a guess, or a threat, or something he said because lots of couples say it. We could actually read each other's minds. It took a while to get used to, and I still got some unwelcome pictures in my head—

("Why are you mulling over cobbling together a tractor/combine/BMW hybrid? So you can get the harvesting done really, really fast?")

--but Sinclair had it worse.

("Please. Please stop thinking that not knowing Burberry made rain boots for toddlers means you're a terrible godmother.")

We clasped hands like mature adults and sedately mounted the stairs, and our reward for behaving ourselves was—

"—like oversexed moles *again*—"

"Yes, but it's a very special day."

—to overhear more bitching. I'd be annoyed at overhearing someone running me down behind my back, except everyone in the mansion says exactly what they think right to my face. All. The. Time. And now here came Jessica, loaded with babies, and our friend/major domo, Tina, loaded with baby gear. She was small (she barely came up to my collarbone), petite (her little wrists were barely an inch across!), and soft-spoken: she'd been a Southern belle before she died just after the Civil War. Or during the war. I don't know; I'm not her biographer.

Anyway, her slight frame looked all the more hilarious since Jessica had basically loaded Tina like a pack mule. She had the port-a-crib, two diaper bags, a mesh bag full of toys...and that was just what was in her right hand and slung over her right shoulder. I wondered if I should warn her about physics. Naw. She probably knew about physics. They had physics during the Civil War.

"Majesties," she murmured, sidling past us to get to the stairs.

"Hope you got splinters," Jessica added cheerfully.

Sinclair's thought was like an arrow: *Friends. The ultimate mixed blessing.*

"Yep." Then I was hurrying down the hall, the absurdly long hall—okay, let me back up, because living in a mansion is amazing. As oblivious as I can be, even I wasn't so laden with privilege that I'd dare complain that my new job(s) required a three story 6,000+ square foot mansion. There were a lot of us, that was one thing. We did a lot of entertaining, that was another. You never knew when random vampires would swing by to give us blood oranges and swear to never try to burn us alive, that was a third. Or when random werewolves would swing by to give us venison and swear to never try to hunt us down and slaughter us. Or when random mermaids would swing by and bitch about the state of the Mississippi River. Or when we'd host a pot luck.

We also needed a lot of security (see above), lots of room to spread out (see above: the mansion menagerie), and it wasn't just our home. It was vampire HQ. Sinclair and I were expected to live like we were large and in charge. Apparently knocking on the door of a two-bedroom condo in South Minneapolis to pledge fealty to the ruler of the undead nation was...anticlimactic.

All in all, good "problems" to have. But today I wished we lived in an RV, or the smallest mobile home ever designed, because getting down the hall to our room was taking *too long*. But then! Coming into sight: our door, end of the hall, like an oasis. A sex oasis.

In half a second we were back in each other's arms on the right side of a (locked) door, and now my outfit was the one that looked like someone had fed it through a shredder, jamming be damned. Especially my sports bra. Sinclair loathed sports bras.

I loathe sports bras.

Yeah? Do you want to walk around with a big band of elastic cinched around your chest for ten hours a day? No? Then shut your fang hole.

How do you make the silliest comments sound unendurably erotic?

I don't—wait. Is that a compliment? Because that's gonna determine how I respond.

Or I could just hold you down and do filthy things to you until you're delirious with pleasure.

...that works.

Sinclair tossed a few more scraps to the floor

(whee! fabric confetti!)

and bent his head toward me. The sting of his fangs breaking the skin over my jugular worked on me like Pavlov worked over his dogs, or whatever the hell he did to them. You've heard "my knees went weak"? My knee bones disappeared. Knee bone? Singular? (Mental note: check with Marc on the number of knee bones.) *Everything* disappeared except Sinclair and his sinful sweet mouth. In seconds he'd pushed me from 'damn, have I ever been this horny?' to "oh, shit, I'm gonna come".

Which is when he pulled back, the bastard, and held me at arm's length. Like he was going to hug me and we'd go our separate ways. Like he *wasn't* going to fuck me, the mere thought of which was horrifying. He grinned at my outraged squeak, his teeth red with my blood, and the overriding thought

(I'm about to fuck a very dangerous man)

had lost none of its power in the five

(six? two?)

years we'd been together.

He put his big hand in the middle of my chest and gave me a gentle push, which sent me flying back six feet

(wheeeee!)

and landing in the exact center of our bed. (Sinclair knew about physics.) Before I could even prop myself up on my elbows, he was on me. His kissed and sucked and nibbled up and down my throat, occasionally helping himself to a sip while I did my best to spell his name out on his back in scratch marks. (Fun vampire sex fact #4: the marks and bites would heal within minutes.)

My love, you define delicious.

S-I-N-K—dammit! Your name doesn't have a K in it. I'm pretty sure...I can't think when you're doing thaaaaaannnnnggg...

Sinclair and his clever clever tongue were doing wonderful things to the shell of my ear while his hand slid between my thighs as I tried to remember if there was a K in his name. It was on the tip of my tongue—oooh, his tongue! Of all Sinclair's yummy collection of parts, his tongue was—

"Uh, Betsy? Sinclair?" A tentative *rap-rap-rap*. "Sorry to bother you, but we need the heating pads."

Sinclair froze in mid-nibble, then turned his head and honest-to-God *snarled* at the door. "Touch that door again and I'll pull your eyes from your skull."

(This is all kinds of wrong, but: *oh my God soooo sexy!*)

I knew the voice. "Not a good time, Will!" Will Jar, part-time blogger and full-time zombie, the latest to join our little clutch. (Our gaggle? Our herd? Our litter? Coalition? Brace?) "It's our special day!"

"Yes, ours too. Um. Sinclair? I'm not actually touching the door—just having a conversation through it—so maybe don't yank my eyeballs out?" Will's voice was calm, measured, and just short of wheedling. "We just need the pads."

I shifted beneath my husband, who was resting his forehead on my shoulder and muttering dark threats into the side of my neck. "Wait, we?"

A fresh bout of hammering actually shook the door in its frame. "Heating pads, you oversexed bimbo!" Marc Spangler, Zombie M.D., sounding a tad—shall we say—peeved? "And yeah, Sinclair, I mean *you*."

Another snarl from the vampire king. "Do you think because you're zombies I cannot kill you? Gentlemen: I have been at this a *very* long time."

Somebody cleared his throat, and then Will piped up with, "Yeah, um, noted, but...your wife would prob'ly just bring us back to life. Again." A pause. "Right?"

"Right," I sighed. "You're not leaving until you get whatever it is you want, are you?"

"Whatever it—I've *told* you what I want!" Little known fact: when Marc lost his temper, his voice climbed so high, dogs all over the block went crazy. "More than once! We could have taken care of this in the kitchen ten minutes ago!"

"Right, right. I remember." To Sinclair, I added, "He wants oven mitts for some reason. He won't shut up about it."

A howl from the other side of the door. "I *never* asked for oven mitts! Heating pads, I want your heating pads and I'll be damned if Will and I are re-bingeing *Game of Thrones* without them!"

"What?" Betrayal! Marc was supposed to binge *GoT* with *me.* Oh, wait. That was *Better Call Saul.* Wasn't it? We needed a bingeing schedule. A vampire queen's work is never done. "Besides, you're already damned. You're a zombie who hangs out in Hell, for God's sake. Textbook definition of damned."

"Focus, if you please, on his reasonable, if inane, request," Sinclair muttered. "Just surrender the heating p—"

"Never!" I'd elbowed my way out from under Sinclair, climbed off the bed, and was on my feet yelling at the closed door. "Those are ours! I'm claiming squatter's rights, Marc Spangler, and you, too, Will Jar!"

"Mason. My name's Will Mason."

Do. Not. Care.

"You get your own!" I finished, relieved because one way or another, this discussion was almost over, and also because I had the moral high ground. I almost never had the moral high ground. I was a vampire, for Christ's sake.

"Those *are* our own!" This punctuated with another flurry of rage hammering. Our poor door! If it buckled under the stress, we'd get a new one for half price. You've heard of cut cards? Get ten haircuts at the same place, the eleventh is free? We have bed cards. "I bought two of them from Walgreen's just before Christmas and I bought three more from Target last month." Thud-thud. Kick. "Want to see the receipts?"

"Oh. I mean, no." Huh. "So...you *don't* want more oven mitts." A peculiar movement caught my eye and I turned to look. My husband was lying face-down on our bed, shoulders shaking with what I hoped was a fit of the giggles. "But you *do* want half a dozen heating pads, all purchased by you?"

"Yes! Jesus, *finally.*"

"Ha!" I was now directly in front of the door; I was about to chastise the *hell* out of the door. The door would not know what hit it. (None of our doors knew what hit them.) "Trick question, we have *eight* heating pads in here!" I'd have mimed a mic drop, but it wasn't 2010. Take *that*, locked bedroom door!

Then the door got demanding: "Give. Me. My. Heating pads."

"You may have half of *one* heating pad."

"Half?" The door wasn't too keen on that, given how it was shuddering in its frame again. *Yikes, hope Marc put on shoes for this.*

"Darling, for the love of..." Sinclair, his giggle fit apparently under control, had gone into the bathroom and emerged burdened with heating pads, trailing cords like they were tails. "There are mere hours left of our special day. Give him the pads and then give yourself to me."

All right, two things wrong with that. One, I was pretty sure I still had the high ground. Two, *he* should be giving himself to *me.* It was only—

"Agreed," he said at once. "Take me. Have me. As long as one of us does something to the other one of us. *Soon.*"

Well then. I reached out, unlocked the door, swung it wide open. "You win, whiners."

"I don't think the plural is fair," Will said mildly, peeking over Marc's shoulder. He was a writer, and they're the worst when it comes to nit-picking language.

"Jeez, Betsy, maybe a robe next time before we're subjected to..." Marc made a vague gesture toward my mostly-naked self. "All of that."

"So avert your zombie gaze," I snapped. "You weren't exactly invited up here, y'know."

"What's that got to do with anything? I hadn't known you a month the first time I saw you naked. In the kitchen, no less! How does someone with your money never have a robe at hand? It's so tacky and hellooooo, Sinclair."

My mostly-naked husband handed off the pile of pads. "Here. With our compliments. And so begone."

I stuck a finger under Marc's nose and his green eyed gaze managed to shift from Sinclair to me. When he wasn't being shrill, Marc was actually great-looking: short black hair, vivid green peepers, about six feet tall, and he looked competent AF in faded hospital scrubs. His sweetie, Will, was cute, too, in a slender blond mild-mannered way. For a guy who sat in front of a computer all day when he wasn't chatting up ghosts, he was in good shape, with lean lines and placid blue eyes. He smelled like clean laundry and was helpful and nice...an example to zombies everywhere.

Now that I thought about it, there were only two zombies in the world, and they both looked terrific. They were a credit to their species! (Right? Species?) Instead of the movie stereotype of rotting corpses stumbling around yearning for brains to slurp, Will and Marc were only one or two minutes dead. Maybe just seconds dead. And instead of devouring brains on the half shell, they needed intellectual challenges to "live". And they'd remain that way—seconds dead, still warm—as long as they didn't stray too far from my side. So there were gonna be zombies living here for a long, long time.

In my younger days (three years ago) when I was a naïve waif, that would have been a deal-breaker the size of Alaska. But I'd had to adjust my thinking on a number of issues since I woke up dead. Betsy Taylor: vampire queen, ruler of Hell, stereotype shatterer.

(I really don't get enough credit for the amazing shit I do.)

And none of it was relevant. So back to the subject at hand: the handing off of the heating pads and the banishing of the zombies. "You got off lucky, pal!"

"I'm pretty sure that's a lie," Marc said, still averting his gaze from my nudeness while trying not to openly drool at Sinclair's.

"Nobody's getting off," Will piped up. "We're taking it slow."

"Yes," my husband sighed. "Quite right. No one is getting off."

"Spare me the grotesque detail of your zombie sexual shenanigans."

"But that's my point," Will continued. "There aren't any, because—"

"Keep up, Will, the topic is heating pads, which you came looking for, and now have, and we didn't have to give you shit, but we did." Again: not enough credit for the nice things I do. "Why d'you want so many?"

"The same reason you do," Marc replied. He'd finally torn his gaze from Sinclair's splendid flank and was winding cords so he could dart off with his horde of heating pads without tripping. "While we're only in the very earliest stage of autolysis, we still can't regulate our cell temperature without outside assistance."

I just looked at him, then blinked slowly, like an undead owl.

"They help us keep warm," Will translated. "For snuggling."

I turned back to Marc. "Next time, just say that."

"Next time, I'll burn this fucking house down around your ears," came the muttered reply, and then Marc was grabbing Will's hand and off they went. Will looked at us over his shoulder and opened his mouth as the door (finally) started to swing shut.

"Sorry to bother y—"

Slam. Click. Fuck?

"*Yes*," Sinclair said, but before he could do the old grab n'toss, I gave him a shove and followed him onto the bed. We tussled like puppies (horny pupp—nope, no, never mind, terrible simile) for a few seconds until I stretched out on top of him. I lowered my head and indulged in a long kiss.

"I don't care if they find a bomb in our basement (again). We're not leaving this room and we're not answering the door for anything."

"Agreed. Now if it won't trouble you overmuch, could you...ah...that? Please?"

I smiled against his throat, took another sip. Marveled for the hundredth time that something that sounded disgusting could feel so indecently amazing. Drinking my husband's blood was like the best drug rush ever coupled with the best brownie sundae ever and the cherry on top was multiple orgasms.

From *one* nibble. Just one.

Pleased with his delighted groans, I kissed my way down his throat, across his shoulders, down his chest. I licked and licked at his nipples—Sinclair's were as sensitive as the cup of my ear was. His fingers were already sliding through my hair and carefully cupping the back of my skull.

There ought to be a law against you.

Well, there isn't. But there are laws against some of the things I do, if that's any consolation.

Surprisingly: yes!

I kept working my way down until I was eye to eye (so to speak) with his cock. Here's something fun: the stereotype about big tall men who have large hands and feet? Totally true. I licked the plummy head for a few seconds

(hhhhhhhnnnnnnggggggg)

and then sucked him in, taking care with my fangs. Sure, we healed pretty instantly, but who wants to risk a fang to the testicle? I didn't even *have* testicles and it sounded terrible. My lips had to stretch just a bit to accommodate him, but given that he was always happy to go down on me for half-hour stretches, I in turn was always happy to return the favor. Well. Maybe not a thirty-minute favor, because if I wasn't bouncing on his cock in another minute, I wasn't going to be responsible for my actions, even the really bitchy ones.

"I know, I know," I said, pulling off, giving the crown of his cock a buh-bye-for-now kiss, then straddling him. "The lack of foreplay—it's gauche. Rushed. Sophomoric!"

"Fine, it's fine, everything's fine, whatever you want is fine, that's fine." (Oral sex rendered my husband incapable of using synonyms.)

"Terrific! Glad you're on board. And technically we've been indulging in foreplay since the kitchen. Interrupted foreplay, but nonetheless...you mind grabbing...?" I gestured toward the drawer beside bed and Sinclair tried to vocalize

"Muh?"

and then groped for the bedside table. My book (I was re-reading my favorite, *Gone with the Wind*...I still remembered reading it for the romance and being kind of amazed to find there was a huge war in there, too), the lamp, and our old-fashioned (it wasn't even digital! old *old* fashioned) clock all hit the carpet, the latter with a jangly thump. For a second I was afraid he'd just rip the drawer out and hurl it across the room, but I needn't have worried.

"Dammit!" he growled, "where *is* the blasted thing?"

He just yanked the drawer all the way out, then upended it, then nearly pitched me to the floor when he moved over to scoop the contents off the floor, and finally tossed it to me in triumph. I caught the tube of a sexually active vampire's best friend (mint chocolate chip flavored), flipped open the top, squeezed a generous dollop into my palm. In the old days, I'd hold it in a clenched fist to warm it a little, but...

Sinclair's sly thought slipped into my brain: *This would be a perfect time to utilize one of the heating pads.*

"Don't even start with that," I warned, but couldn't stifle the giggle. "And brace yourself."

He let out a hiss as I slicked him up, and nearly leaped off the bed when I squeezed his length while running my lubed palm over and over and over the head of his cock. One of those don't-stop-wait-too-much-don't-stop sensations. (I felt the same way whenever I wolfed down a DQ Peanut Buster Parfait.)

I leaned forward a bit, he leaned up a bit, and then his thick cock was filling me exactly the way I liked: hard and inexorable and so, so fine. I pressed my palms against his shoulders and started to rock back and forth

(ah God that's good)

as I took from him exactly what he wanted to give me, which was everything. "Christ," he gasped, gripping my hips hard enough to bruise, and I leaned down for another kiss, nibbling on his lower lip and teasing him with my tongue.

More.

"Yes."

Harder.

"Yes."

His hands left my waist and cupped my breasts. I leaned down so he could kiss and lick my nipples, so he could whisper dirty glorious things into my cleavage, so I could feel him smiling against my flesh. We delighted in each other, there was no other way to put it, and we lived for these moments when we could indulge in an act made joyful as much by what we said and were to each other as by the physical part.

"You. Are. Glorious." Each word was punctuated by an upward thrust.

"Yes," I agreed. I gripped the headboard to steady myself as I rode him. "Which works out nicely, since you are, too."

He smiled up at me, his dark gaze never leaving my face. *My own, I should be dead without you.*

"We've done the dying thing. It's passé. Good thing we got it out of the way early, huh?"

Only you could make returning from the grave—on multiple occasions—sound like filing your taxes in January.

This time on the upstroke I didn't go right back down, so only the tip stayed inside me. I kept us there for a couple of seconds and smirked as Sinclair cursed. I didn't have the upper hand for long—my smirk was premature—because Sinclair seized my shoulders and rolled, and in half a second I was on my knees, eye-to-eye (so to speak) with the headboard as he eased his cock back in.

"Whoa," I managed, and grabbed headboard as he set a punishing/amazing pace. I braced so I could push back and was rewarded with a groan.

"Christ."

Yes.

"You are exquisite, my own."

Yes. Harder.

He tightened his grip on my hips and obliged, and I knew I'd have five little bruises on each hip when we were done. Those bruises (all the sex bruises, really) were the only ones I wished would linger.

I dropped to my elbows, was rewarded with another deep groan, and reached back so I could stroke his balls with two fingers (my arms weren't quite long enough for a real grab).

"No," he gritted out. "You. Touch yourself. I'm...close. Stroke your clit for me."

So bossy. Still, it was an order I was happy to follow. *Stroke your clit* was right up there with *try on the allllll the shoes.* So, obedient creature that I was, I slid my hand down between my legs and skated my fingers over and around and alongside my clit, again and again, and I didn't have the words to describe how gdslkdgjlsg lskdg;a llksdg laskgd;alk llsdgj;;

You're close, too, my own, darling queen. You're getting tight all over. It's hhhhnnnnnnggggg

"Less thinking," I gasped, amazed I was able to vocalize. Everything was getting brighter—like our room was lit by rheostat and someone was turning it all the way up—while the sensations had narrowed to my fingers and Sinclair's cock. "More fu—ah!" A sensation not unlike leaping from an airplane and falling into an orgasm blanked my brain, and even as I was trying to think/say/beg 'don't stop', he wasn't. He fucked me through it until there was nothing but white noise—no, that was Sinclair, who was usually discreet but now and again didn't give a shit if someone heard him roaring out his orgasm.

In the movies there's always this tender moment between lovers who have just banged the bricks loose. They gaze into each other's eyes or manage breathless declarations of love and/or fidelity as they shiver in each other's arms with just the slightest sheen of sweat on their gorgeous perfect bodies.

Since this was real life, I released my grip on the headboard and flopped prone, mumbling a breathless declaration of love and/or fidelity into my pillow. I might have drooled a little.

Sinclair flopped down beside me and chuckled. "*La petite mort* is wholly inadequate."

"Gmmmff umph," I replied. Also: a tiny bit more drool.

"And we still have three hours left of our special day."

That motivated me to flop over until we were facing each other on our sides. "I can't believe you remembered."

He'd reached out to smooth my bangs out of my way, but paused. "How could you think I would forget?"

"Because normally you give not one shit about that stuff? Hey, I'm not complaining. It was a great day."

"Agreed."

"I finally—"

"Happy anniversary, my own darling queen."

"—got my hair the exact shade of red—what?" *Oh, fuck.*

In a panic, I sat up. "No," I said, trying not to lose my shit. "No! Our anniversary is months, *months* away."

He reached out, caught my arm, pulled me in close for a snuggle. "Calm down," he murmured into my (newly red) hair. "Your heart is hammering."

"Yeah, sure, it's probably pounding away at ten beats a minute. Listen, I didn't forget our anniversary." For one, Tina would have never let that happen. I'd had to actively prevent her from buying a gift for him, ostensibly from me ("I only wish to lighten your burdens, Majesty.") more than once. "I think—I think you're a little mixed up." Or senile. He *was* over a hundred years old.

"No," he murmured, stroking my (newly red) hair. "Not the meaningless government ritual you insisted we practice. Our first wedding, our true wedding."

I wriggled until my kissable hair was out of his reach. "True wedding? Dude, if you're getting me mixed up with some floozy you hooked up with during the Great Depression..."

"You know you're the only floozy for me, dearest."

"That's a relief." I was too sated to give him a well-deserved pinch for turning floozy back on me. "So then, what...?"

"The pool. The fight. The Fiends. The ignoble end of a tyrant, the start of our glorious reign."

I mulled over "ignoble" (and tried not to giggle at "glorious", because he sounded like a Russian propaganda poster) and then I had it: he meant the swimming pool "wedding" that took place within days of our first meeting. How could I have forgotten?

Serious question. How could I? I saved Sinclair's life that night. I cured his fatal burns. We killed the bad guy and then fucked, naked and upside down, in the deep end of a random swimming pool. When we came up for the air we didn't need, we were—hey, presto!—the new king and queen of the undead. Such were the rules of undead matrimony and monarchy.

(Hey, it's no weirder or inconvenient than a destination wedding.)

"We belonged to each other from that moment."

I snorted. "Which was awkward, since I hated you back then."

"No," he said smugly, and that time he *did* get a pinch. "And your hair is lovely. But you must know I wouldn't care what color or length your follicles were."

"Ooh, I love your sexy follicle pillow talk."

"The we are well matched for that if nothing else. And we have some time left. We—oh."

Yeah, I heard it, too. Now that we weren't focused on getting laid, we were a little more aware of the world around us. There were at least two sets of footsteps coming down the hall, followed (natch) by a knock on our door.

"Betsy? It's Mom. BabyJon caught some kind of bug, the poor thing just barfed all over his car seat."

Offer her a heating pad.

Oh, very funny. It could have been worse. She could have knocked ten minutes ago and I would have had to beat her to death.

"I wouldn't be bothering you—"

"Of course you should bother me, Mom," I called, hunting for clean clothing that wasn't shredded. "He's my brother/son."

"—but Marc and Will were adamant that you would want to be notified at once. And Tina and Jessica backed them up."

"Because of course they did," I muttered. "I'll be right down."

Sinclair was still lolling on the bed; he looked like a Roman general, post-orgy. "'Uneasy lies the head that wears a crown.'"

"Not so fast, co-monarch, your head's uneasy, too. He's your brother-in-law/stepson. C'mon, give me a hand."

"At once," he said agreeably, because he was a modern centenarian and hip to feminism. He rolled off the bed and to his feet, then began his own search for a shirt that hadn't been reduced to cotton confetti. "And I have been remiss. How could I have gone most of this day without telling you I love you?"

"Because you suck? Which is literal *and* figurative." Then I hit the pause button on Sarcasm Mode. "I love you, too."

"Because of course you do."

I grinned. "Because of course I do."

Five minutes and a quick wash later he presented his arm. "Shall we?"

"You're gonna escort me to a puke-covered car seat?"

"But of course."

I had to shake my head at the hilarious absurdity. We were co-monarchs who routinely cheated death (or co-opted death for our own ends) when not hoarding heating pads, squabbling with our friends, and sponging up puke.

What the hell, I took his arm. "Lead on, sir."

And he did.

THE END

MY ANGEL IS MY DEVIL

by

MaryJanice Davidson

PART ONE

This is insane. Going with a stranger to a hotel room?

`He's not a stranger.  We've had coffee together.`

You stood in line behind him at Starbucks and ogled his ass!

`But` *what* `an ass.`

And he caught *you ogling.*

`I know.  God, that grin.  That dimple!`

This again? That's why we're here to bang a Starbucks stranger you've met a few times? We didn't even see his driver's license!

I don't care about his driving
record.

You get that you're basically advertising that you wouldn't mind being murdered, right?

Shut up.

Do you know how many crime drams start like this?

D'you know how many great pornos
start like this?

"Enough! I can't get into the right frame of mind with both of you yammering in my ear."

Sorry.

Oh. Sorry. Um. Frame of mind?
Easy. Just plug in the vibrator and
start without him.

Yes! The vibrator! You don't need him; we do fine on our own.

Lilith Tien, who had been fruitlessly taming her tangle in front of the bathroom mirror, had to squash the urge to hurl her brush at something. And not just to shake those two up a little. To punish the brush.

"You guys heard me shriek 'enough', right?"

That shut them up. Finally. Lilith closed her eyes, took a deep breath, then opened them and...ugh. Still a nightmare on size eleven feet. Straight black hair that resisted even the slightest wave. Desperation had demanded she get it chopped to a chin-length wedge. But that showcased her premature gray hairs, as trapped by her hairbrush. Her treacherous hairbrush.

And while the cut was an improvement, there was still the matter of the rest of it: small brown eyes a little too far apart, mouth a little too wide, boobs a little too small, feet a little too gross.

See? You're almost never this hard on yourself. You need this, we all need this!

"No."

You know you're perfectly pretty, you just need some—

"I'm not fucking a coffee acquaintance as a confidence booster," she snapped. "So let's derail that train of thought right now.

—orgasms.

"I have tons of orgasms," she protested.

Orgasms in the presence of another person. Just to see if you like it!

Wait. That's a good point, you've never been shy about plugging in Mr. Shaky—

"It's upsetting that you've nicknamed my vibrator."

—so why are we loitering in a Minneapolis Marriott hotel room to fuck a—

With perfect timing, there was a discreet rap-rap on the door. Since she'd been in the middle of reapplying make-up, she nearly coated her nose with Sonia Kashuk's *Very Berry*. She dropped the balm and fixed herself with a stern glare in the mirror.

Oh, look! It's The Look! Please, you're not impressing anybody.

Nothing wrong with an expression that shows you mean business.

Unless it's purely for show, which this is. You've still got time to call it off.

DON'T YOU DARE. Remember that ass. You deserve this! I believe in you!

"Coming!" she called.

Oh, God, I hope so.

We'd better, after all the trouble we've gone to. We'd better come twice. Perhaps thrice.

"Cut it out, you two," she snarled. "I'm not kidding."

Well, I'm not going to say anything.

`Ha!`

But you know I'm upset.

"Then *be* upset. Silently upset. Stoically upset."

She stepped out of the bathroom, took one last glance at her outfit: knee-length black skirt, bare legs, no shoes, short-sleeved red sweater that did wonders for her complexion. She definitely had a glow. A good one, not the "I think I have a fever" kind.

Why did you spent three hundred bucks on clothes that will be on the floor in a couple of minutes?

`Don't listen, Lilith...`

She snorted. "I've been trying to ignore you for how many decades?"

`...we look terrific!`

She took a last look around at the lighting scheme. Bathroom light was off. Closet light was on. Desk lamp was on. Overhead light was off. Bedside lights were out. She hoped she'd hit the middle ground between operating room bright and witching hour dark.

King-sized bed. *En suite* bathroom, which was just a fancy way of saying you didn't have to hoof it down the hall to do your business. Nice big closet. Nice big television (that she hoped stayed off all evening). Functional desk. Decent view of downtown Minneapolis in the fading evening light, which would look even better at night. (Probably, she'd closed the curtains.) Neutral carpet (tan with brown specks). Functional, non-offensive, comfortable.

Are you gonna keep staring around the room?

She wrenched the door open, and her future one-night stand recoiled. She could have bitten her tongue, instantly chagrinned. "Oh! Sorry."

"Wow." He held up his hands in mock surrender. "Are you going to smack me? I don't think we negotiated that."

Oh, if only. I'd like to smack him into next week.

Will you give him a chance?

"Sorry," she said, feeling exquisitely stupid. Two seconds in, and she'd already embarrassed herself. A new personal best. "I was just—" Arguing with the angel on my right shoulder and the devil on my left. Nothing to see here, just typical pre-one-night stand stuff. You don't mind if I talked to my imaginary shoulder cops while we fuck, do you? One of them is going to be relentlessly critical and the other is going to be relentlessly enthusiastic and it's going to be exhausting. "Um." Oh, excellent. Clumsy *and* inarticulate; who could resist her?

"Actually, I'm really glad to see you. Here, I mean." He gestured to the room. "I was wondering if, uh."

She found a smile, which was something that wasn't at all difficult when she talked to Seth Gabriel, and was one of the reasons she'd chosen him to help break her dry spell.

"If I was going to chicken out?"

"Well." He shrugged and it was adorable. He had a way about him that was bashful yet confident; he'd shrug and smile and then peek at her through his long eyelashes, lashes that were wasted on a man.

His dark blond hair was long (like Tom Cruise in *Mission: Impossible—Ghost Protocol*) but not too long (like Tom Cruise in *Mission Impossible 2*). His eyes were hazel, rings of light brown around pupils that faded to green, and a dimple bracketed his mouth whenever he smiled. He had a plush lower lip that she wanted to bite every time she saw him, which was not a socially acceptable way to greet someone you'd only seen at Starbucks.

They were exactly the same height, five feet ten inches, which was the first thing he'd commented on when she dropped her Green Tea Frappuccino on his feet a month ago.

Exactly! A month! You barely know him!

`I can't believe it took me a whole month to talk you into this.`

He was wearing tan slacks with a black leather belt, and a crisp white button down under a dark blue blazer. Dark brown lace-up Oxfords and black vintage-style glasses with clear lenses completed the look.

She'd always been a sucker for a guy in glasses. When she was a middle schooler she'd had a crush on Clark Kent, *not* Superman.

"Lilith...may I come in?"

She almost groaned; she'd kept him in the hallway while she drooled over his glasses and thought about nibbling that full lower lip of his. So she overcompensated, swinging the door open so wide, the handle slammed against the closet door. They both jumped. Mercifully, the mirror (all hotel closets had mirrors for doors; it was like a state law) didn't shatter.

"Aw, jeez." Over. It was all over before it began, and yep, another personal best.

"Hey." Seth had taken one of her hands in his. "It's okay. I mean, I'm nervous, too."

"I'm not nervous."

Lie.

"I'm mortified," she continued.

Truth!

He laughed, a sexy chuckle that started somewhere in the middle of his chest and rumbled up and out. He could have the body, complexion, and flexibility of a haystack and she'd still be attracted to that wonderful deep voice. "Y'know, we don't have to—I mean, we could just hang out and watch a movie and have midnight hot fudge sundaes and take a bunch of Buzzfeed quizzes, if you want."

Wow! Great!

Wow. Nightmare. Buzzfeed? Seriously? YOU WON'T BELIEVE WHAT THIS QUIZ SAYS ABOUT YOUR SEX LIFE! Ugh.

"Seriously?" She wasn't looking for an out, but she was surprised he'd given her one within sixty seconds of seeing her.

On cue, the bitch on her left shoulder piped up (again): *Why are you surprised? He's obviously ready and willing to call the whole thing off. Don't wait. Take him up on it. NOW.*

Noooooooo!

"Nooooo," she said. "I don't want—I mean, I'm glad you're here." She stepped aside and gestured for him to come in, like a maître 'd in a push-up bra showing a customer to their most mediocre table. "Let's stick to the plan."

"Whatever you want, Lilith. Did I tell you, I love your name?"

He loves our name!

Oh, please. He's not just a pick-up, he's an unoriginal pick-up. He's—what? Two years away from thirty? And he's stuck on 'derp, great name!'?

"I know." She could feel the blood rush to her cheeks. Did that sound vain? It was hard, sometimes, walking the line between confident and conceited. "I mean...you said. About my name. The day we met. You said. My name? You liked it. My name, I mean."

You know what? I feel a lot better about this. Your innate inanity is going to chase him right out of here.

"The hell it is!" she snapped, and stepped forward, put a hand on the back of his neck, and brought his face to hers in a clash of teeth that was barely a kiss.

"Nnnnnnfff!"

"Oh my God." She reeled back and saw a tiny drop of blood well on that beautiful pouty lip. "I'm so sorry!"

Oh, Lilith, what did you do?

Ahhhhhh-ha-ha-ha-ha!

Maybe he likes a little of the rough stuff. Quick! Swoop in and do it again so he thinks it's on purpose!

Ahhhhhhhhhhhhhh-ha-ha-ha-ha!

Mortified, she buried her face in her hands, but at his chuckle she dared to peek. "You should be running. Seriously. Save yourself. This will only get worse. I've accidentally set myself on fire. Twice."

"Lilith Tien, you don't scare me," he replied, and stepped in close.

Then he is a foolish, foolish man.

ZOMG, so sweet!

His hand as it cupped the back of her head was gentle. So was his mouth as it slanted over hers, as he gave her the nicest, sweetest kiss she'd had in two years.

"Your mouth," she managed against said mouth, and pulled back a bit. "D'you know how many times I wanted to knock your iced espresso out of your hand and just kiss you and kiss you and kiss you?"

He smiled. "I would have been startled, but into it. But think about those poor scandalized baristas!"

"Let 'em get their own gorgeous nurse." She thumbed another drop of blood away, and he kissed her thumb. Which was fine. They'd exchanged STD panels four days ago.

At least you haven't completely *lost your marbles.*

`Safety is the new sexy!`

She initiated another kiss and they spent the next couple of minutes making out like teenagers after prom.

How would you know? We didn't go to prom.

`Don't make it sound like we couldn't get a date.  We had mono again.`

"You—um—" She tugged at his shirt. "Make that go away."

Oh good God.

`Yes!  The shirt must go, ALL OF THE CLOTHES MUST GO.`

"Your wish." He stepped back and began unbuttoning his shirt and she quickly realized what a terrible error in judgcment she'd made.

"No."

Yes! She sees sense! Finally!

"Please. Let me." Lilith couldn't remember the last time pushing buttons through holes had been equal parts erotic and satisfying. While she unbuttoned, he rested his hands on her waist and kissed the tender spot behind her ear.

I hope he doesn't spend too much time on our ears.

`I hope he spends HOURS on our ears!`

It's hard to think when his tongue is gaaaaaaaahhhhhhhhhh...

"Oh, that's nice," she sighed as he turned his attention to her throat, flicking his tongue as he licked up to her other ear.

...aaaaaaaahhhhhhhhhh...

"I love your throat. And I love the little beauty marks right over your jugular."

...aaaaahhhhhhh—what? Idiot. Those aren't beauty marks—

`Yes they are!`

—they're a type of melanocytic nevus.

Lilith was now sliding his shirt off his shoulders and tipping her head back to allow him more access.

`Well, he definitely told the truth about being a swimmer.  Those shoulders!  And his back!  He's just a walking pile of lean muscle mass.`

Fine, he told us one thing that turned out to probably be true (maybe). This is still reckless with a dash of stupid.

`YOU'RE reckless with a dash of stupid!`

Really? That's your comeback?

Seth pulled her shirt over her head while she wriggled out of her skirt, chuckling as she clutched his forearm to keep her balance. No need to make it more awkward by accidentally giving herself a concussion. "Yeah, yeah," she managed. "Warned you. I'm a mobile disaster."

"'Disaster' isn't exactly the first word that comes to mind when I think about you. And I do think about you, Lilith. All. The. Time."

Creepy.

`Romantic!`

"I can't even tell you how happy I am that we're both here now. All week I figured you'd come to your senses and call it off."

That was a vain hope, Seth. A VAIN FUCKING HOPE.

"You could be with anybody," he continued as she backed him toward the king-sized bed and fumbled for his belt buckle. "Literally anybody."

Figuratively, Seth, you braying idiot.

`Shut the hell up, grammar police.`

Right. Because expecting people to know what they're talking about is such a high bar.

"But you picked me," he continued, oblivious—thank goodness!—to the turmoil in her brain. "Just some random nurse you sometimes have coffee with—"

"With an angel's name," she said, smiling. "And there's nothing random about you, Seth Gabriel."

"—but you! You work anywhere you want, you set your own hours, millions of people read your work—"

She tried to squash it, but the giggle bubbled out anyway. "I love how you're making it sound like I have a real job with real world impact."

It IS a real job.

Fortune cookie writer is not a real job. "Your co-workers are definitely talking about you behind your back" is not a fortune. "Tomorrow will suck harder" is not a fortune.

We pioneered funny fortunes, dammit! Why are you always so negative?

"It pays the rent," Lilith said demurely. Mostly. She supplemented by writing greeting card verses.

(Roses are red.

Violets are blue.

Your ass is so fine.

Your dimple is, too!)

"Why would you even pick me?" She was still fumbling with his belt and he took her hands in his, squeezed lightly to stop her. "I never talked to you. I mean, I noticed you. Everybody did, probably, you're so—"

Bedraggled?

Alluring?

"So..." she prompted, and she wasn't fishing for a compliment. (She wasn't!) Merely being courteous, giving him a chance to finish his thought.

"Well, you know. But I didn't really talk to anybody."

"Introvert," she teased, and was he...? Yes! He was actually blushing a little.

So. Frigging. Cute.

Maybe he's having a stroke.

"I am, yeah. I was really glad you dropped your Frapp on me. Instant ice-breaker."

Instant lawsuit.

"I was glad, too." But only in retrospect. She didn't even know what she tripped on, which was the story of her pratfall-filled life. She didn't know what her victim's reaction was going to be, either, but assumed it would be negative. This was the land of Minnesota Nice, but you could push some people only so far, and not one step further.

She only knew that her drink went flying and she was stuck on a greeting card verse because everything that rhymed with 'doodle' was ridiculous and thank goodness she'd avoided spilling on her shirt because she was out of detergent and it was par for the course because it was only Wednesday.

"So you didn't spill your drink on purpose?"

She burst out laughing. "No. In fact, I do that about twice a week."

"So you weren't, uh, luring me into your web of seduction with your Frappuccino-esque wiles?"

Words failed her and she laughed harder as Seth's blush deepened. She remembered—was it only a month ago?—being horrified to see green goo slopped and oozing all over his shoes. His expression: startled, then cautiously pleased. He'd put her at ease almost instantly, explaining that as an ER nurse he was immune to being grossed out by...well...anything.

And before she knew it, he'd bought her a new Frapp and they were chit-chatting about their lives.

So here they were, and it was hard to remember how nervous she'd been ten minutes ago, and with that thought, she reached for his belt buckle again. Was there anything sexier (besides dimples) than the sound of a man unbuckling his belt? That 'clink-clink' went straight to her clit. "D'you want to know why I kept coming back to that Starbucks? The one ten miles out of my way?" She'd been getting an oil change, then went to Walgreens to kill time while scoping the competition's greeting cards. Which made her thirsty, so: to the coffee shop!

His blond brows arched. "Really?" he said, delighted. "But I saw you there at least half a dozen times!"

"Well, sure. Because I kept coming back. Because: the dimple."

"Noooo. That's amazing! My grandma was right."

Really? REALLY? He's gonna drag his Nana into this? What kind of a depraved freak talks about his grandmother while seducing a hack?

"She predicted your dimple would be like catnip?"

"Yeah, actually."

"Better call her up and tell her she was right."

"She died six years ago."

"Oh." She took her hands off his belt, because yikes. "I'm very sorry."

"She'd been sick for a while. It was sad, but not unexpected."

If I can't talk you into leaving, can we at least speed up the seduction? Pretty please? Also, STOP TALKING ABOUT DEAD GRANDMOTHERS.

I hate to be negative, but she's actually right. I mean, it's sweet and all, about his poor grandma, but it's not conducive to passionate lovemaking.

Or at least, it'd better not be.

"Enough about your dead grandma." Oh my God. Had she...? Yep. She'd said that out loud.

Out.

Loud.

She must have look stricken, because he smiled and said, "It's okay. I know what you meant." His hands went to her waistband. "May I?"

Yes. For God's sake, a thousand times YES. Let's get this freak show back on track. Its laughable careless dangerous weird stupid track.

Except for the mean thing at the end, I agree.

"Oh, yes, please." In a few seconds he had her stepping out of her skirt and was skimming her shoulder blades with his fingers, pushing her bra straps down, and reaching behind for the clasp. This gave her access to his neck, which she kissed and kissed and kissed as the bra went, as her panties went.

At least you didn't wear the Cookie Monster underpants.

Target has remarkably sensual lingerie!

She got hold of his belt again, the holy grail of belts, the most wonderful of belts, and then she thumbed the button open and yanked the zip.

"Okay, I'm feeling a little rushed here, but it's okay, since that's pretty hot."

"Less talking," she teased, "more undressing." His pants puddled around his ankles, and...

Here's a tip: shoes, then belt, button, zip, pants, socks, shirt. In that order.

It's going great! You've got
this.

He grinned and opened his mouth to reply
and she lost patience with the whole damned
thing because *honestly*. She planted her palms
on his (broad) chest and shoved; his back hit the
bed as she got her fingers under the waistband
of his black boxer-briefs.

Boring.

Classic!

She wasted no time tugging them down and,
for the first time, got a good look at his cock.

God DAMN.

Whoa.

"Oofta," she managed, and he giggled,
which should have been absurd coming out of
that deep chest, but wasn't. "You've been
keeping secrets."

"There never seemed to be an appropriate
time to introduce the topic," he deadpanned.

Good one. Dammit.

Just when I thought Seth Gabriel
couldn't get yummier...

Don't say 'yummier'. We're not thirteen.

I'll say whatever I like! And what's your problem, exactly? All you've done today is be a pill!

And all you've done is be insipid.

Shut up!

YOU shut up!

"Stop it!" Lilith shrieked, and Seth nearly fell off the bed.

"What? Are you okay?" he asked, sitting up and peering down at her with wide eyes. "I'm so sorry, whatever I did—"

"Nothing!" Everything, her two inner idiots were ruining everything again, *again.* "I mean, you didn't do anything. You're fine. You're beyond fine. I just—" She made a fist and bopped herself in the right temple. "Please don't read into this but every now and again I can't shut off the hubbub in my brain and I was scared to come here and I wanted to come here and I couldn't wait to come here and every morning I looked forward to seeing you and I've never done anything like this before and I guess you could say I'm of two minds about it..."

Yep.

At least!

"...but I want this. I want you. I just—"
How? How to explain that her cheerleading idiot
and her dour bitch—

Hey!

`Rude.`

—that her angel and her devil, who (to be
fair) looked out for her, and tried to help her even
if their methods were beyond irritating, got louder
and shriller and harder to tune out the lonelier
she got?

Nope. There was no way to explain that.
Not without sounding hopelessly unhinged and
in dire need of anti-psychotic meds.

"Hey." She looked up to see Seth had
scooted down to the edge of the bed, had leaned
down and cupped her chin in his hand. "It's fine.
It's all fine, Lilith, I promise."

Fine. The perfect word for mediocrity.

`Give him a chance, jeez!`

"I had seven brothers and sisters. My mom
worked two jobs and I was so obsessed with
quiet and privacy I ended up seeing a therapist
because you know what? We're all a little nuts.
No exceptions."

She sat back on her heels and studied him.
Calm. Comfortable. Not weirded out in the

slightest. And that was such a relief to her she was almost dizzy with it. "Is that why you became an R.N.? Because you know what it's like to be the one who needs help?"

"No, I became an R.N. because any time one of the eight of us had to present to the ER, the nurses were incredible. Nothing phased them. Not even when my sister bled on them and then—because blood freaks her out—threw up on them. Twice!"

Annnnnnnd we've moved from talking about dead grandmothers to talking about bleeding barfing siblings.

`I hate when you're right.`

"Okay." She took a deep breath, nodded. "Thanks, I feel a lot better."

"Happy to help."

"And how long are we going to pretend that your dick hasn't been bobbing between us for the last twenty seconds?"

It's like a flesh-colored baton!

`So hypnotic.`

"As long as it takes!" he declared, "and then we ggggnnnn ohhh my God."

She'd grasped his cock at the base, gently squeezed, then licked a stripe from balls to crown. It was fair to say she had liked his cock on sight and liked it even better close up. She trailed kisses from the flushed red crown to his perineum and back up while Seth fell back with a delighted groan.

Finally! Down to business.

No thanks to you and your constant negativity.

Lilith let out a warning growl—

Okay, okay. We'll be quiet.

Like church mice!

Church mice? Out of all the things in existence that are quiet, you went with church—

And here comes the negativity, right on cue!

—and then another growl, this one louder.

Fine.

Okay.

Fortunately, Seth took it as something she'd meant to do as a means of titillation—

"Ahhhhh, the vibrations when you oh *God,* that's good!"

—as opposed to her having to break off to squash yet another internal mutiny. She sucked his cock back into her mouth and felt the spongy head hit the back of her throat. She felt one of his hands settle in her hair and peeked. His right hand was clenching the bedspread so hard his knuckles had gone white, but his left was gently resting on the top of her head.

She popped off, which elicited another groan, and said, "You can pull. I like it."

"Jesus," he managed shakily.

"And you can thrust in and out, nice and hard, if you want. I like that, too. I haven't had a gag reflex since I ate a bunch of nightcrawlers in fifth grade on a dare."

"So you're just effortlessly perfect in bed. That's what you're telling me. Perfect."

All right. Gotta give it to him. Anyone who hears the worm story and thinks 'perfect' is worth getting to know.

Shhhhh!

Sorry! Sorry.

He did start thrusting, then, but the hand in her hair never clenched, never wavered from gentle caresses. "God. God. Your mouth, ah, *Christ,* your mouuuuuth...stop. Stop."

She backed off at once, rested her hands on the tops of his thighs and looked up at him. "Are you okay? Did I—"

"I'm miles beyond okay. Okay is missing the mark by a huge margin. C'mere." He reached down, caught her by the arms, dragged her up off the floor, onto the bed, onto him. "It's been a while for me, is all, and you're so—I don't want to be done in sixty seconds."

"We could stretch it out to ninety seconds, if you think you're up for it," she teased.

"Oh, very funny." He rolled them over until he was on top—yay, king-sized beds!—and kissed her, explored her mouth with his agile, clever tongue, worked his way down her throat, to the tops of her breasts. He licked at her nipples, nibbling around the edge of the areola and flicking the peak with the tip of his tongue, which was ohhhhh so nice, because her last boyfriend had treated her breasts like chew toys. Toys he was very, very fond of, but still: chew toys.

She broke off from her thoughts, anticipating her angel or devil piping up with their $0.02, but...nothing. They were apparently keeping to their agreement.

"That's lovely," she sighed, cradling his head. He was nibbling at the undersides of her breasts, now, and paused to reply.

"The underside is actually much more sensitive than the top. Right here, just above the inframammary fold—"

"Oooh, love the dirty talk. Now talk about ligaments and glands." She squealed as he pinched her.

"It'd serve you right if I did," he mock-warned. "I know tons about glands. Gobs."

"That'll learn me," she agreed. "I—ack! I'm a little ticklish there."

"Here?" he asked, and then pressed noisy kisses all around her belly button.

"Yes, aaggh!"

"Here?"

"Yes! And I think you know it!" She would have kept up the giggling/scolding, but he'd settled down to business and after nuzzling her pubic hair (she'd decided to do a Brazilian, then had a 'fuck it, I am what I am' moment, then compromised with a bikini wax), licked and sucked kisses all over her inner thighs. In all the years she'd been sexually active (four), men just *dove* down there and went right for oral, as much for their own benefit

("Boy, you're super wet! Time to fuck!")

as, ostensibly, hers.

But Seth was in no rush, it seemed. He'd made himself a nice little temporary home down there and caressed and kissed and nuzzled, and when he (finally) parted her and probed with his tongue, she wanted to weep in relief. Up to that point, she'd been groaning into a pillow she'd snatched up and held to her face until

"Please don't, I want to hear you, I'd love to hear you..."

she'd tossed it aside and just...just *writhed* on the bed with nothing on her mind beyond seeking out more stimulation, more friction, more anything.

Five minutes later, she was ready to yowl in exquisite frustration and raw *want*. He'd varied parting and probing her with his tongue with soft leisurely licks, occasionally sweeping across her clit, then settling back to more flicks of his tongue. And he was teasing her with his fingers as he did all those things, sometimes holding her open with his thumbs as he licked and kissed, sometimes running two fingers up and down and occasionally over her clit, only to pull back and lap at her with broad sweeps of his tongue.

"Jesus," she groaned, and was that her voice? So thick and slurred? "Seth, please fuck me. I never thought I'd say this, but that's enough foreplay." She could feel how wet he was making her, could feel an ache burning through her from head to heels. "I want your cock, Seth, c'mon."

"Oh, but it's so nice down here," he murmured. "You've gone all slippery-soft and the *sounds* you're making, Lilith. I could almost come from those alone."

"Don't. You. Dare." She reached down and tugged at his shoulders and he came up into her arms and she kissed him. Kissed him and tasted herself and pulled one of his thumbs into her mouth and sucked while his dark gaze never left hers. She reached down and found his hot hard length, felt him throbbing impatiently against her palm and *God*, he felt good.

"How?" she said. "Tell me. On my back? On my hands and knees? On top, riding that fucking gorgeous cock of yours? I want any of that. All of that. Tell me."

She could almost see his I.Q. drop along with his jaw. "Oh, *Christ,* that's—I—wh—uh—on your back, this time? I want to see your—I mean—wait. I'm not assuming—I wouldn't want you to think I'm getting ahead of myself—or taking you for granted—"

She nibbled on his lower lip and ran her fingers up and down his hot, slick cock and he shivered against her. "Shut up. Fuck me. And there'll be a next time. Count on it. So just ahhhhhh!"

She wanted it, was more than ready for it...and it was still overwhelming in all the best ways. Nothing hurt—he'd made her *so* wet for him—but the sense of being filled was astonishing.

And it only got better when he started to move, long deep strokes in and out as he put his palms on her knees and spread her a bit wider. She met his every thrust, clutched at his shoulders, then balled her hands into fists—her nails were long and she was afraid she'd claw him to ribbons as she chased her pleasure.

"Lilith. You can. You can do. Whatever the fuck you want. To my back. Okay?" Each pause was punctuated by a stroke so hard and deep she practically felt him in her throat.

"That's so good," she slurred. "You feel so good, please, harder."

"You're incredible," he groaned, "you—please tell me you're close."

"I—"

"Because I might die if I try to hold this off. And also, please tell me that speed turns you on."

She laughed, then cut herself off with a gasp. Close? Oh, yes. He'd edged her into the sweet spot, those last few moments between wanting to come and knowing it's inevitable. She found it hard to believe they'd been talking about his dead grandmother fifteen minutes ago.

Don't think about that now, you silly bitch!

Good advice. And she was so close, even those two yammering away couldn't muck it up. She was sort of amazed they'd stayed quiet as long as they had.

FUCK, he's good at this.

`Fuck!  He's good at this!`

Ah. That would explain it. Wait—did that mean all she'd ever needed to keep them quiet was really terrific sex?

She couldn't think about now. The only thing she could think about was... "Don't stop," she managed. "I'm so close, I—ah—" The warmth that started in her belly now raced through her and the world fell away as her orgasm crashed through her. She could hear someone calling out hoarsely

("Seth-Seth-Seth-SethSeth*SethSethSeth*—")

and realized that, unless it was Seth's habit to scream his own name during orgasm, it was her. She locked her ankles behind his gorgeously muscular back as he fucked her through it, as he stiffened just seconds later. She saw his eyes roll back and then he was shuddering through his own climax and collapsing, rolling to the side at the last moment so he wouldn't squash her under his full body weight. (Which, for the record, she would have been fine with.)

Nobody talked for a long time.

Which was *great*.

PART TWO

They spent the night together, which was lovely and unexpected for both. When they'd made the agreement last week, they confirmed that either party could leave at any time for any reason.

But Lilith—who hadn't dare hope for anything beyond a vigorous half hour of lovemaking with no hard feelings if they never saw each other again—found the thought of getting dressed and leaving unsupportable.

The best part? She wasn't the only one.

"Are you kidding?" Seth had asked. They were still coming down and enjoying the afterglow; Lilith was on her side, one of his arms around her shoulders while he stroked her hip. "D'you think this happens every day? Because I sure don't. You're lovely and I knew that before I saw you naked—also, you look *so good* naked—

but the last thing I want to do is leave. And it's nothing to do with sex."

"Nothing?" she teased. And that led to great appreciation for Seth's refractory period, which was apparently under six minutes. And greater appreciation for the deep pleasure of slicking him up and riding his cock while he gripped her hips and fucked up into her and groaned and wondered out loud how he'd gotten so fucking lucky.

They had room service dessert at midnight (crème brûlée for him because he loved pudding, chocolate mousse for her because chocolate), showered, drifted off together.

In the morning she woke to him kissing the back of her neck as he stroked her left breast, brushing his fingers over the nipple until it had stiffened beneath his palm. His hands and mouth were everywhere, silently asking permission, and when they were both panting he coaxed her over on her hands and knees and took her from behind, all the while gasping things like "beautiful" and "wonderful" and "perfect...Jesus, your ass is *perfect*".

She'd been gripping the slats of the headboard, then dropped to her elbows and smirked when he groaned. She rocked back against his cock, impaling herself while urging him to go faster, harder, begging him to fill her and fuck her, and when she came he made a low noise behind her and followed her over the edge.

They showered again. Dressed, packed, left the room. Looked at each other while waiting for the elevator.

Now what?

Shouldn't we fill the silence? I don't want it to get awkward again.

Unnecessary; Seth broke the silence. "I'm not going to ask you out."

She blinked at him. "Thanks for letting me in on your plan, I guess." It was fine, wherever this led, whatever he meant by that. She just knew, somehow, even if she didn't understand why, or where that surety came from.

Seth smiled and took her hand. (The one holding her overnight bag, which was a little weird, but okay.) "I'll go home first. I'll think about you all the way home and while I'm unpacking. I'll think about you while I'm checking the hospital schedule so I'll know when I'm free. I'll ask you out then, so you won't think it's something I'm saying just now to break the awkward post-bang silence."

She giggled at 'post-bang silence'. "Seems prudent."

"I won't ask you out now so that when I ask you out later, you'll know it's real."

Damn. I'm starting to like this guy.

`'You'll know it's real', swoon!`

She stared at him as the elevator dinged, followed him on. "Whether I see you again or not, you're a marvel, Seth, did you know?"

"Well. *Now* I do." Pause. "Are you impressed with my convincing attempt at modesty?"

"Not in the slightest." She kissed him again, thinking that even if was for the last time...

It won't be.

`We'll track him down like a dog if we have to!`

A well-hung dog with dimples.

`And now you've ruined dogs. And dimples.`

...it had been an unforgettable night.

PART THREE

Seth Gabriel pocketed the receipt—Lilith had insisted they split the room cost—and headed for the parking ramp. Lilith. Christ, just thinking her name made him want to grab for his phone and call, call, call: can I see you tomorrow? And the day after? And forever?

He'd promised to call her from home. Since he spent a lot of time in his car—argh, the commute!—didn't that count as home? Sort of? Practically the same thing, right? Or was he reaching? And what if he *was* reaching?

Stop obsessing.

No way! If anything, he's not obsessing enough. We gotta swoop! It's a fucking miracle she's even single!

He sighed and rubbed his temples.

Gotta hand it to you, she was great.

Great? Damn her with faint
praise much? She was incredible!

Hey, I said I was wrong, didn't I?

No. You didn't, actually.

*Fine, you fucking baby: I. Was. Wrong.
About. Lilith.*

Thanks, shithead, was that so
hard? And watch your fucking mouth.

"You guys," he groaned. "Give it a rest.
Can't we just...bask in the wonderfulness of the
last fourteen hours? Quietly?"

Boring.

Naw, it's sweet!

*But don't bask too long, pal. Women like
that aren't exactly falling out of the sky.*

"One in a million," he acknowledged. "And
then some."

On that, they could all agree.

THE END

MaryJanice Davidson is the best-selling author of several novels, including the UNDEAD series and the BOFFO trilogy, and is published across multiple genres. Her books have been published in over a dozen languages in fifteen countries, and have been on best-seller lists all over the world, including USA Today and the New York Times. She has published books, novellas, articles, short stories, recipes, reviews, and rants, and writes a bi-weekly column for USA Today, who were kind/foolish enough to give her a national forum (http://happyeverafter.usatoday.com/author/mary janice-davidson/).

A former model and medical test subject, she lives in St. Paul, MN, with her husband, children, and dogs. You can reach her at contactmjd@comcast.net, follow her on Twitter (@MaryJaniceD) and Instagram, find her on FB (https://www.facebook.com/maryjanicedavidson) and check out her blog at http://maryjanicedavidson.blogspot.com/.

Or you can steer clear entirely. No hard feelings either way.

Made in the USA
Middletown, DE
26 April 2020

91378373R00083